DANCING WITH SNAKES

Gladys Swan

DANCING WITH SNAKES

Gladys Swan

Serving
House
Books

ISBN: 978-1-947175-02-0

Cover art: Painting by Gladys Swan

Serving House Books logo by Barry Lereng Wilmont

Published by Serving House Books
Copenhagen, Denmark, Florham Park, NJ

www.servinghousebooks.com

Member of The Independent Book Publishers Association

First Serving House Books Edition 2018

Thanks for Marina Marcello for her editorial proofreading.

For Pep & Shirley

"Just as the snake must shed its skin, we must shed our past over and over."

—Gautama Buddha

I.

Lights all a-dazzle. Dancing across the marquee like a comet's tail. That's me. Amazing. Featured act here at the new Las Vegas nightspot—Galactic Explosions, the latest shows a play of colored lights and images that whirl your mind to worlds beyond imagination. I get to show my stuff here and in Atlantic City and Miami too, plus an offbeat little place in L.A. The rest of the time I travel with the circus, where I'd rather be. The glitz pays the bills and allows me to save up for my education. My great dream is to go to college and discover other worlds there. I've got lots to learn; I have to make up for lost time.

So tonight I'll step out onstage in my favorite costume, red and gold, sequins and rhinestones on the outside, me on the inside. Then with well-timed consideration, I remove my veils and girdles and get down to the real thing—me in my bikini, giving a shimmy, getting the parts moving before inviting the snakes to appear. There's a gasp from the audience—count on it. That's my cue. And I'm on, doing my dance.

What a way to earn a living, you say. But I'm off into the excitement that holds me breathless, moving with the snakes as they move with me, and maybe you'll get caught up in the wave, into the thrill and fear that clutches at the midriff—that takes you to the edge.

Amazing all right. But that's not the half of it. Even more amazing is how I got here in the first place, counting all that happened along the way. And I'm not here for keeps. I'm biding my time. There's a special person I'm waiting for, to come and tell me his story. Meanwhile, hang on, and you'll know all.

Snakes? Some people are scared spitless by the very mention of them, let alone having one crawl over your skin. Once I read about the Hopi Indians, how they gather snakes and let them crawl all over their bodies as they sit in the kiva, calm and steady as a cedar post. Then they dance with them—rattlers and sidewinders, with their

9

fangs and poison. They call them "Brother." And after the celebration, they let them go.

Though I, too, felt a stab of fear at first, I came to feel a kinship. Like they lived inside me. Whatever drew me towards the snakes lived in my childhood before I was able to reach for words to tell about it.

When I was a kid, I hardly had a name. It felt like I was kin to animals. Maybe that was on account of something you couldn't give a name to—a wildness that lived in us both without my seeing any difference. I just preferred to get down under the table with the dog or the cat, or go chasing after a rabbit in the weeds.

There wasn't a whole lot then to tie me to the human. I couldn't remember anyone calling me by a syllable that drew me to the sound, made me want to take it on. Oh, I might hear, "Hey you," or "Get on over here, you little stinkweed." This from the one who stood in for a father, if he stood anywhere at all. Not that I ever called him Daddy. A mouth, that's what he was, all scrunched up like he'd bit off too much of life and wanted to spit out the taste before he choked on it.

His name was Priam Gillespie. He hated that name, the way people pronounced it Pry-am or Pree-am. Every once in a while somebody would say, "What the hell kind of name is that?"

"It's what comes of having a librarian for a mother," he'd explain. "Damn her hide anyway."

Every once in a while, maybe in a store or the bank, somebody would call him Mr. Gillespie, and I'd look around for the stranger I thought they were speaking to. Sometimes he called me Miss or Missy. "Don't give me any of that guff, Missy." Or "Toots" when I was coming on to being a woman. "Oh, so now you're getting ready to strut your stuff, eh Toots." I wanted to kick him.

Somewhere there was a birth certificate with my paper name but it just fell by the way—it had nothing to do with me. Whenever somebody spoke it, I didn't look around or say a word. "What's your name, honey?" some folks would ask, and when they drew a blank, they'd smile down into my face, as if getting closer would turn on the light bulb, and ask, "What's your dolly's name?" It wasn't a real doll, just a sock with stuffing in it, and button eyes and a mouth sewed on.

"Name," I'd tell them. "Name—that's her name?" That would tickle them all right.

And Priam would say, "She's just ornery—always has been." Maybe Ornery could have been my name.

"Just wait till I can send you over to Texas," he'd say every once in a while, like he was trying to get even with me—"and let that mama of yours do what she was created for." And then under his breath, "If she'd quit running around long enough to do anything useful."

A voice from long ago ran like a tune through my head: I could remember someone holding my hand. I could almost feel the way it curled around mine—warm and a little moist—even when I couldn't attach a person to it. Was that my mama? I couldn't see her—I was never sure. I really couldn't remember any mama at all. Seems like I'd just happened in this place, like a scrap of paper blown in by the wind.

Every once in a while I'd ask when I was going to Texas, but Priam would pull a face and say, "Mind your business. I got troubles enough as it is."

It took me a while to get a name, as I'll tell you, and it happened in a way I never expected. That seems the way of things—full of surprises. My life started changing when I was about eleven—when Priam got hold of a piece of land across the highway. Took it for collateral from a Mexican family who'd got into his clutches.

I used to play horse with their kids, and Carolina and I liked to braid each other's hair. Hers was long and black and glossy, and I loved to get my fingers in it. Sometimes I'd eat dinner in their adobe hut—tortillas with beans, and enchiladas with red chili sauce, and sopapillas with honey. I can almost taste the food yet—the chili hot in my mouth, then the sweet taste of the sopapillas—and the way Carolina's mama filled my plate and teased me and treated me like one of her own kids. The day they all left, I stood there like a stone, watching them pack up their truck with boxes and baskets, lifting up the couch, then the kids piling in, lining up on it, their dog in the middle, a friendly brown mutt with a long body and little short legs named Chico, who was always part of our games. Then they were gone in a cloud of dust.

"Vaya con migo. Vaya, amiga. Muy lejos de aqui." Let me grab my stick and trot my pony—ta da, ta da, ta da.

Their adobe hut sat empty for I don't know how long, the wind shuffling a few tumbleweeds and scraps of paper in its direction. A little way off were some dilapidated sheds and corrals that had once kept horses or cattle, plus an abandoned shack that people said was haunted by the ghost of Geronimo. I never figured out what he'd be doing there in the neighborhod unless he was really down on his luck. But us kids had played like he was still inside and whoever saw him gave out a yell and took off. I never saw him, but I pretended I did and yelled and ran with the rest.

Just opposite was our place with its peeling adobe and rusting truck parts and junk scattered around the yard. Priam outside lying in the hammock or sitting in a rocker that no longer rocked, wearing down the day crabbing about the heat or cussing the dog or kicking the cat, whatever had the misfortune to cross his path, while a few dusty chickens pecked at what they could come by among the weeds.

One day after a cloudburst had turned the yard to mud, a beat-up black truck pulled into the ruts at the edge of the place, and a fellow unfolded himself from inside and made his way around the mud over to where Priam was sitting under the box elder, the only shade—a scrawny fellow with a high forehead, cleft chin, and a snaggle tooth when he grinned. He stuck out a bony hand to offer a handshake and said, "Howdy, I'm Tiger Higgins and I hear you own that piece of property there across the blacktop."

Priam looked him up and down. "What's it to you?"

"I got a business proposition—that's what."

"Prime land. Make you a fortune in the cattle business," Priam fired back. "I been waiting for the right investment."

"Looks to me like a grasshopper would starve over there. But I'll make you an offer you can't refuse. "

I could tell Priam didn't believe a word of it, but the smell of a deal set the juices flowing. After a session of jawing and jockeying, sweating and swearing, the two of them landed in roughly the same spot, and afterwards Priam even offered the fellow a shot of whiskey.

Money changing from somebody's palm into his own always pumped him up for at least three days.

A couple of weeks of feverish activity—tearing out rotted posts and boards, hammering and nailing, repairing sheds and fence posts, putting up metal bars and attaching chain link fence and the place looked pretty good. Then a sign went up. Roadside Zoo—Animals from the Wild. Exotic. Thrilling. The Jungle brought to your very doorstep.

The jungle—in the midst of that stretch of yucca and cactus and mesquite. The idea seized hold of my imagination—the biggest thing to happen since third grade. Once I'd learned to read and do arithmetic, Priam figured I had all the learning I would ever need to make my way in the world. The rest you could get from TV—though ours offered up mostly snow and static. Meanwhile he'd find enough to keep me busy.

I wanted to hang around and watch the goings-on—and a couple of times Tiger let me hand him nails and tools—fun stuff—while he told me about tracking animals and how you had to show the big cats who was boss. But after a couple of days Priam came and fetched me home.

"He ain't open yet, Missy—you can do a look-see later on." So I watched from the other side, when I wasn't taking care of the chickens or sneaking off to the arroyo to look for rocks with fossils in them. I found a neat book once in the school library showing creatures that had once lived when the world was new and the mountains were the bottom of the sea.

One day I got to go over and pick up the beer cans and whiskey bottles and paper cups and pieces of plastic that had been tossed out from passing cars and landed in each other's company. Tiger paid me a dollar and a half and gave me a soda. The place was beginning to look halfway decent.

The next day a big trailer-truck pulled up. Tiger and a couple of helpers, a high school kid—big square fellow, Greg—and the other, Ralph, older but strong, who acted like he knew about animals, opened up the back and started unloading cages and crates and leading out the animals. They hefted a cage with a tiger onto a trolley, then another, with a young one, hardly more than a kit. I'd never seen a real live tiger before, never seen wild animals up close. And here came a leopard, an ocelot, a cougar. I got goose bumps all down my arms.

Then came the dog types—coyote, fox, and dingo. Some of the animals were new to me—I had to learn what they were. They led a camel into the yard, who passed it over with a sneer. I could see monkeys, even a zebra. There were birds too. A couple of gaudy parrots, a big white cockatoo. Finally some wooden crates labeled "reptiles."

Lights had been strung up along with the signs. GRAND OPEN-ING. Special family rate—little kids free. For a while things were hopping. People pulling in to look at the zoo and stop at the stand to buy a soda, some chips or popcorn, or get a bag of food for the animals. "You get folks involved," Tiger said, "—keeps down the overhead that way." He tapped his head to show how full it was of smarts. When the place closed up for the day, Tiger came over with a bottle of whiskey, and he and Priam poured it out into two orange juice glasses and lifted them to the future.

Tiger had a gold mine, nothing less, and he was full of plans now that he was on his feet again. Bad luck a while back with some of his animals over in Oklahoma. But he'd bought up a new supply from a couple of zoos selling off their surplus and their elders. Now he was going to breed tigers again—He was waiting for the young female to get to where he could breed her. Once he'd bred over twenty tigers—that's how he'd got his name—and sold them all to folks that practically stood in line for one of the kits. A huge market for all he could produce. "You can't imagine—all the folks wanting their own tigers—and ocelots and leopards, but especially tigers." He was one big cockeyed grin, and the two of them kept at that bottle till they were chummy as blood brothers.

After I'd nagged him till he was ready to tear his hair or mine, Priam took me over to see the animals. The cages were all lined up, the cats all together, the monkeys in their own spot, and the coyote, fox and dingo—dog types—in theirs. It was the little tiger that won my heart. I stood in front of her until I could feel Priam's impatience coming at me in a hot blast.

I hated to leave her. She just sat there looking around, bewildered, uncertain, like she'd found herself in a strange place and didn't know what to do. I could tell from her eyes.

The other cats acted like they knew exactly where they were and kept pacing from one end of their cages to the other. No wonder. Hardly enough room for them to turn around. The lion was in a different space—didn't budge all the time we were there, just lay in the sun with eyes half-lidded.

More action with the monkeys. They were moving all the time. Each had a swing, but they couldn't swing very far, so they took to hanging and swinging all along the sides. The parrots sat on their perches picking at their feathers. Every once in a while the cockatoo let out an ear-splitting shriek.

"Let's go home," I said. My head was full of noise and smells, and I had a sinking feeling I couldn't give a name to.

"Now hold on," Priam said. "You had ants in your pants to get over here. And I got to see to my investment. I want a look at what's inside."

Inside were the reptiles, and a slimy smell. A big turtle sat on a little pile of dirt in a circle of stones, a pan of water nearby. To keep it company a pair of rattlers were draped over a dead branch not far away. Then in the next tank I saw a circle of thick coils spiraled around until they pointed forward into a dark head with a white stripe in the middle. The coils had wiggly black and yellow strips that made a pattern. Beautiful to look at, but it made me dizzy and sent chills down my spine. I held my breath.

"That's a python," Ralph said as he was setting things up. He'd just finished putting a heating pad under the tank. "Carpet python. How'd you like that for a pet?"

I could feel something coming from inside it that nobody could claim. Different from the cats. I felt I knew them as soon as I laid eyes on them. All their fierceness. Proud. Dangerous. But I had the feeling they knew how to dream. I wanted to get to know the cats. I wasn't sure about the snakes.

The python just fixed me to the spot, not giving anything away. Looked like it was curled around something calm but cold, like nothing would dare to bother it. Made me feel how jittery I was.

"If they trust you, they're easy to handle," Ralph said, maybe to reassure me. "Only you have to be careful. If they're hungry, they'll strike at anything that moves and throw their coils. The big ones can kill a man."

He would have gone on talking about them, but Priam hauled me off so that Tiger could show us the rest of his critters, as he called them. We threaded through the kids with their popcorn and sodas and bags of animal food, and their moms and dads. But I'd seen all I wanted, and kept pulling at Priam's arm till he was ready to slap me. "Go on home then," Priam said. "You make me tired."

"Wait a minute," Tiger said. "Come on over here. We'll give you a treat." He led us up to the soft drink stand and asked me what I wanted. "This one's on me."

I didn't want anything, but something told me I shouldn't say no. We stood for a moment watching the big kid I'd seen before, who stood behind the counter trying to add things up and make change for a family who'd bought drinks and popcorn and animal food. He was having a slow time of it.

When they left and I'd settled on a root beer, Tiger and Priam stepped back a ways to talk, while I watched one of the spider monkeys picking lice from his partner, and pretended I wasn't paying any attention to them. I always kept my ears cocked—I've learned a few things that way.

"Be good for her—give her something to do. Instead of being a plain damned nuisance."

"Pretty young to be putting money in her hands."

"She's a whiz, I tell you. Can make change like a cash machine. And that kid you got there running things . . . not too swift up there in the cockpit. Probably stealing from you on the sly. And come September . . ."

That's how I got my first job.

"Get you used to earning your way in the world," Priam told me.

"Pay for your board and keep. It's owing to me right enough—all I've had to put up with." He made a face like he had an ache with nothing to cure it, and I went off to work the picture puzzle the social worker gave me before she moved away.

I was good at fishing the sodas out from the ice chest and filling the little packets of bread crumbs and bags of limp lettuce and vegetable tops and fruit Tiger collected free from the groceries to sell to folks that wanted to feed the animals. And I was good at making change. I got to keep two dollars of it every week after Priam took his cut. I put it in a little purse I had to keep it from the damp and hid it down near the arroyo under a special rock.

Things were pretty busy that summer. People pulling in to see the jungle at their doorstep. And since it was hot and dusty, they bought lots of sodas. I liked talking to people and hearing where they came from, and I'd look at the kids and try to imagine how it was to go traveling with moms with lipstick on and shiny purses and tall, good-looking dads, mostly with nice teeth, and friendly smiles and cameras hanging around their necks.

When nobody was around, I'd go visit the animals because neither of us had anything much to do. And Ralph would tell me stories about them. He'd worked a lot with elephants and big cats, and he'd take me on his rounds and tell me about his days traveling with a circus.

"That's really exciting," I said, ready to be excited by just about anything.

"It's an interesting life," he said. "I liked being around the animals, especially the elephants. You get close to them. And I sure didn't like the way they were treated. They can be awful cruel in the way they train animals in some of those big circuses. The trainers showing off for the public." He let me take that in.

Of course I'd never seen a circus and it sounded like a whole other world. It sounded like something magical.

"Animals have a lot to offer," he said. "If you listen they'll tell you things. I swear it." I was ready to try for it.

Sometimes he was all jittery, complaining about Tiger and the zoo setup. Too crowded. And Tiger was skimping on the food. "Those guys—I don't understand them. Why aren't they in real estate? They don't know what the hell they're doing. You think they care anything about what's sitting inside those cages?"

I tried to keep my eyes open to see how the animals were doing. The little tiger always looked glad to see me. They didn't have regular names—just a label like Bengal Tiger with a piece of Latin underneath. I tried to get to know the animals. I started talking to them, and it seemed like they were listening. Sometimes I'd sit real still and go over a bunch of names in my mind and see what came to me. Then I'd try out different names on them. Gave me something to think about. I could tell the big male tiger liked Caruso, even though I tried Hercules and Elvis.

It took a long time to get to know about the kit. Ralph liked to wrestle with her, just play with her like any cat. And he let me play with her too. I loved her. But mostly she was in her own space and a lot of the time seemed to be thinking or dreaming. At first I thought she was like a fairy princess who'd been stolen away from her land and home and turned into a tiger that had to wander for years till she was rescued from the wicked magician who'd betrayed her.

But then Ralph told me she came from somebody's apartment, where she sometimes slept in her owner's bed. It seemed more like she'd forgotten how to be a tiger, Ralph said. He didn't approve of keeping wild animals for pets. "Wild animals ought to be wild," he said.

I called her Antoinette.

"That's just right," Ralph told me. "She's lively and lovely—and that's what it sounds like. They need names—lets them know who they are." Then he muttered to himself. "Which is a hell of a lot more than some people know."

Antoinette liked it when I played with her. Ralph gave her a stuffed owl to bat around. She lay on her back, holding it in her paws, and raked it with her hind feet. "Disemboweling her prey," Ralph said. I knew what he meant. The owl didn't last long. He put in a couple of cardboard boxes and she had great fun leaping into them and sitting there like she'd found her spot. Sometimes he'd put a collar on her and take her out for a walk on a leash. He'd let me hold onto it. He made me be real careful—didn't want me taken by surprise or getting clawed or bit.

"They don't mean to be rough, but they got claws and teeth. They're still wild animals. They're ruthless, cats are, even the domestic ones. I figure they're thinking all the time about the bird or the mouse they're going to catch. Only that's not all of it," he went on. "They can be affectionate too. And everything they do is beautiful. Just watch how they move, how they sleep—in curves. All of them. Beauty and grace and playfulness—all of it together make them what they are—cat." He looked at me. "Yes. Cat. Think of that."

It really struck me, what he said, like he'd put something in front of me that was missing from my life and that I'd have to discover. Even though I couldn't really speak to it or know what it meant, I did try to be on the lookout for it. Even in our old tomcat, Hank—what he was.

The tigers were a big draw at the zoo, but it must have been hard just lying around with nothing to do except let people gawk at them. I could at least roam around a bit.

Ralph kept saying, "I got to get out of this place." I could see how it was getting to him, seeing the way things were going. I couldn't think of anything to say that would help matters.

On the animal side the camel was maybe doing the best, though I knew his legs were bothering him from arthritis, just like Priam's, and he was feeling droopy and irritable. He'd sit for long hours in the sun with his legs folded under him. I came up close just once and he gave me a look as if to say, "Don't even bother." He looked like he was going to spit. Ralph never let the kids on his back—just on the burro and the Shetland—and that was a good thing.

In the afternoon the yard was blazing hot. No shade to move to. The sheds weren't much better. And even the projecting roof boards of the stalls didn't help much. The animals just kept pacing till they'd had enough. Then they flopped down and shut their eyes and slept and kept on sleeping.

They didn't eat much either. Most of the stuff Tiger collected from restaurants and groceries wasn't healthy food for them. Fit for the crows, and Ralph would throw half the stuff away. Then one morning, when Ralph gave Tiger a piece of his mind, the two of them started yelling at one another, and the way Tiger was waving his fist, I was afraid they were going to duke it out. But suddenly Ralph got all quiet, kind of dangerous-looking, and turned and stalked off.

"Asshole," he muttered, and shot Tiger a nasty look over his shoulder. He didn't show up for a couple of days, and I worried about him. Tiger went around swearing and cussing, he had to do all the work himself—even had me running around.

He jumped all over Ralph when he finally turned up. "Where the hell have you been? Are you working here or not? I oughta fire you."

"Just go right ahead," Ralph challenged him. "What'll you do then? I'm only here on account of the animals."

"What d'you mean? I've given you a chance . . . Who else would give you a job?" Tiger backed off.

But Ralph went dark and angry and just glared at me and wouldn't answer when I spoke to him. I had to work to keep back the tears.

Then he came to himself when he saw my face and told me he was sorry. He grabbed me up in a hug. "Oh, I'm so sorry, Sweetheart. Do forgive me. It isn't anything you've done. Just me and my bad mood." Then he hugged me again. "You're my best girl—always." Then I couldn't hold back.

Because I had to do something, I took some of my money and bought hamburger to give to Antoinette and Caruso. Then because it wasn't fair to the others, I saved up and bought enough cheap hamburger to give all the cats and dogs a treat. The meat they were getting wasn't all that much and not all that good. A lot of chicken near the end of its career and scraps of beef or pork the butcher had trimmed away—some of it starting to smell. Caruso would sniff it and stand there of two minds. If he was hungry enough he'd eat it. He was getting thin. Sometimes he'd sit and pull out pieces of his fur.

"You're too beautiful to do that," I told him. "Please listen."

"It's a crying shame," Ralph said. "He earns a living off their backs and he treats them like dirt. All cooped up in that little space. At least give them a good feed. Give 'em good meat and plenty of it. Horsemeat to fatten them up. Ever hear a big tiger purr? Like a motorboat." I wanted to hear that.

The animals took hold of me. I knew how unhappy they were. I couldn't stop thinking about them. I carried them on my shoulders like a weight of bricks. They padded into my dreams and roared and bellowed. They scratched and bit and clawed each other. Their fierceness was sharp as hot needles that drove into their own hides. I could hardly stand it.

"The animals are getting sick," I told Priam.

"Well, Miss Smartie Pants, they oughta put you in charge, you know so much."

What can I do? I asked them.

Set us free, they pleaded. Their cages were all locked up. But just suppose they were let out. What would happen then? They seemed to sink back deeper into their bodies as though they wanted to forget they were alive. The dingo, coyote, and fox were so thin you could count their ribs. By the end of the summer, the parrots had plucked out so many feathers they looked scruffy as old carpet and sat on their perches like they'd been stuffed. All their spirit had leaked away into the air—whatever they had of beauty and grace.

Tiger himself seemed to be losing his grip. You'd see him one moment and then he'd disappear, taking off in the middle of the afternoon, leaving everything to Ralph and me. He wouldn't show up till after Ralph closed the place up for the day. Then he'd slouch in to count up "the proceeds," as he called them, add up every dime, frown as he paid us once a week, put the rest in his wallet, and march off. Some days he looked at us like we were to blame for the thin pickings. Maybe he thought we were stealing.

One afternoon when nobody was around, I found Ralph among the reptiles, taking the python out of his tank. He put it around his shoulders and let it crawl down his chest. I sucked in my breath. I could hardly stand to watch. I wasn't sure what to think about that.

"You want to try?"

I wasn't sure, but something in me wanted to do it.

"I don't know," I said. "It looks creepy." When I was little, a centipede came crawling up my leg once when I was in bed. I screamed like something was about to kill me. But now with the snake, something in me wanted to try. I stood debating.

"I bet you don't scare easy," he said. "You can do it. You don't want to startle them. They got to trust you."

I wasn't sure—I wanted not to be afraid.

I had to look around inside for a quiet spot. I took a couple of deep breaths, then Ralph lifted the snake up to my shoulders, and it came on around. It was an odd feeling at first, something like that crawling on me. It wasn't slimy at all, rather silky in fact. At first I held still as a tree trunk. Then I held out my arm and the python came down my arm and around my waist. I was tingling all over, and I felt happy too. Ralph grinned at me. It was like I'd passed some kind of test.

"You like that, huh? They don't take much bother, but you got to keep them the right temperature. Neither cook them or let them freeze."

I was hardly listening. I was replaying all the sensations, knowing there was fear still there, a dark place beyond anything I knew. And something else—different, but I couldn't say what it was.

It seemed like Ralph's mood had changed, as though he was trying to give me the best of himself. I spent time with him whenever I could, helping him feed and water the animals, so I could hear his stories.

The last one he told me lay closest to his heart—about the one circus he loved, where he handled a half-grown elephant named Tillie. "Came to us as an orphan right out of Africa. Poachers shot her mother. She grew up with me. We loved each other. She'd curl her trunk around me, give me a hug."

A small outfit in Missouri with only one ring—"A glorious circus," he told me, as he described the acrobats, the Cossack riders and their feats of horsemanship, the Flying Wonders on the high wire, the jugglers and clowns, and Lola, who rode the elephant. A whole parade leapt up before my eyes. It was like I was there. And the more he described, the more I wanted to be in their midst.

"Color and lights and music," he said. "Skill and daring. Think of putting yourself out there—taking the risks in spite of all the dangers—plus bad days and small audiences . . ."

I'd never seen him so excited. His eyes lit up. His forehead glowed. Even his bald spot gave off a special shine.

"They were the best—one big family," he said.

"Why did you leave?"

"Like I told you," he said, "it was a small outfit. They did things on a shoestring. Then too much competition—TV, films, sports. They had ten good years. And those were the best of my life."

After that I never heard Ralph complain. He just kept things to himself and did his rounds like a robot. He got a bad cough, bronchitis, and was gone for more than a week. I really worried about him and about the animals. Tiger again had all the work to do himself. He needed help, especially with the cats, and brought in some guy, Eddie, who acted like the whole place was a bad scene and quit after three days.

Tiger had a distracted look. Now there were times when he let the water bowls go foul or empty and I'd drag out the hose and try to get water to the animals. It was hard work. Since he knew I was doing it, he just let everything drop into my hands.

The animals kept visiting me at night—pacing up and down. *This is a prison*, Caruso groaned. *We're dying here*. In my dream I did my best to comfort them. *When I grow up, I'll bring you all home and give you good food, and there'll be lots of room where you can run and be free*. It was no use. *We are dying into our freedom*. I'd wake up breathless and scared, but I didn't know what to do. Once I sat up yelling. The animals were lying all around me in scraps and pieces. I could hardly recognize them.

"Some of the animals aren't doing well," I said to Tiger.

"They think they got privileges," he snapped. "Full of themselves— that's what, just because they perform for the public. Never saw an animal yet that didn't want to up its standard of living." He strode off, muttering. "They think they got troubles."

One of the troubles he probably wasn't expecting was a big dark-haired woman who pulled in one afternoon and stood over me like a tower, then spoke out in a deep voice that had no nonsense in it. "What are you doing here, child, and who runs this outfit?"

I could hardly find my voice. "Mr. Tiger Higgins."

"And where is this Tiger person?"

"I believe he went into town, ma'am."

"And left you here by yourself? Outrageous." She wrote something in a notebook she was carrying.

Since school was in full swing and hardly anybody was coming in, Tiger left me in charge when he went off in the afternoons. Ralph came in when he felt up to it, but he wasn't working whole days. Often Tiger brought back the smell of where he'd been, and I didn't want to get near him.

"Just tell anybody looking for me that your dad's gone to town for supplies," he told me, "and he'll be back in a jiffy."

I didn't want to tell that kind of lie. And I couldn't have told it to her. She didn't offer to buy a ticket but started walking around among the cages, inspecting the place and writing things down. "And what's your name, honey?" she said, when she came back.

I didn't want to tell her everybody called me Missy, even when I'd gone to school. And I'd left behind my paper name that nobody ever used. Something struck me though. I had named the tigers and the other animals, all except the python—I wasn't sure about him yet—why couldn't I name myself? I could call myself anything I wanted. It struck just then what exactly I did want.

"Grace," I said. Just pulled it out of the air. "My name's Grace." And even as I said it, I knew it was a secret thing, and I'd be telling it only at the right moment.

"It's a good name," she said, looking me over. She started to say something, then just muttered, "the jackass." She put a card down on the counter and said, "Give this to your Mr. Tiger." Then she put away her notebook. "Well, darling," she said, smiling a little, "with a name like that I'll bet you'll break out of whatever cage you happen to land in. Just you remember that." Then she was gone.

I spent the rest of the afternoon mooning and dreaming, trying to figure out what she meant. When Tiger turned up two hours later, wobbling as usual, he glanced around and said, "Not much business, huh? How come you didn't sweep up?" He jerked a thumb towards where the brooms were kept.

"My job's behind the counter," I said and went back to the magazine I'd been studying.

"Oh shit," he said, and walked away.

II.

I know about trouble—how it works up slow into a head of steam, things getting tossed in along the way, building and building, till it zonks you before you can turn around to see what's been following in your tracks. I've never been able to figure things out. Somehow you never get the full picture, not even after you've been blasted out from under and the sky is falling, and your pockets are empty and you're trying to pull out just one thread and figure out where it goes and what's at the end of it. Only there's never a beginning—just a bunch of other threads and knots. Maybe the trouble is getting born in the first place. You just land inside a life, bawling and kicking, without knowing where you came from, maybe not even knowing who your parents are.

And according to Priam you're the trouble that just got everything started.

"You ain't got no folks," Priam told me when I tried to ask about my mama and daddy. "You got a grandpa and that's me, and you're lucky you got that. Just remember. And I don't want any more of your questions, you little . . . you've been trouble enough."

Like Orn'ry "Trouble" should've been my name—because whatever lives inside me keeps pushing me on in spite of myself, just making me want to throw myself onto the floor sometimes and squall and kick and make a fuss.

So here comes Tiger, back around, right away looking for the trouble I happen to be sitting on. "You got a funny look on your face like you ain't even here. Anything happen while I was gone?" Tiger said, after he threw his glance around and circled back to me.

"Nothing to tell about."

But he was onto something that drew his eyes to a point, needle-sharp. "Somebody been here?"

"Just a woman—a big tall woman. Taking a look at all the animals."

"Oh, that's it, is it? And what's that laying there?"

"The card she gave me." I'd been studying it, saying her name over and over and thinking about what she'd said and wishing I'd just followed along after her. Crazy, I know. I'd just laid the card at the side of the counter without good sense, fixing to take it home with me. I didn't have a pocket to put it in.

"Gimme that." He read it, then tore it up. "Coming snooping," he said, as I watched it going into little pieces.

"Just coming round and butting in to other folks' business. And look at me—just a hardworking guy trying to keep body and soul together and give folks some good entertainment. Damn those mothers to hell." And he let out a string of cuss words that would have given Priam real competition. "Let 'em come. I'm a citizen ain't I? I pay taxes when I got the money. I know my rights."

Ralph, who'd just come in, had been trying to beat down the cuss words—for my sake I guess. But I knew them all, could have added to the poetry. It was an opportunity Ralph had been waiting for. "If they get after you, it's your own damned fault. There are animal lovers out there."

"Well, they can join up with the faggot lovers, and the spade lovers and the spic lovers, and all the goddamn lovers they want to . . ."

You could practically see the steam hissing out of Ralph's ears. But he didn't get side-tracked—wouldn't have done any good. "Just take a look at the animals. If you don't take care of them better, you'll lose them. And then where'll you be? That's what it comes down to."

"What d'you think I hired you for? You're supposed to be the expert." Tiger stormed off—he had things to do.

Ralph was swearing under his breath. It was the animals that had kept him there. He was the one to do things the right way. Cleaning out their cages and really seeing they got what the needed. Tiger always banked on that. This time Ralph held on like a bulldog and told Tiger he'd have to pitch in and do things right or he'd be doing them all on his own—he was ready to walk. Ralph had made his threats before, only the animals drew him back. This time Tiger knew he meant it. Ralph made a list for him of the supplies he needed in town, and though Tiger didn't get all of them, and still brought home stuff he'd got for free, the animals had better food for a while. He brought back some horse meat and a sack of bones for the cats and the dog types.

"No sharp bones in there?" Ralph said. "You gotta be careful."

"I got good ones—" Tiger said, "even got a little meat on them. You have to pay for all that stuff. They don't give nothing away any more." He handed the stuff around. His treat. There was a lot of gnawing and crunching.

Only the day after she'd had her treat, Antoinette started acting like something had knifed her in the gut. I ran over to see what was the matter. I saw right away her water bowl was empty and I called out to Tiger and Ralph, who were out back with the camel and the zebra. "Come quick," I said. "Antoinette . . ."

Tiger came running up. "What's the matter?

"Come quick, I think she's got something wrong with her belly." I grabbed up the hose while Tiger ran on ahead of me.

When we got to her, she was rolling around sobbing and gasping, snarling at us when we came close. Caruso was pacing and snarling. They had to get Caruso into another cage before they could tend to her. Ralph lured him with some meat, and Tiger maneuvered him with a pole into an empty cage. "You got to go for a vet," Ralph said. "She's in a bad way." He took her bowl and held it out to her while she crawled over and lapped up some of the water, then she flopped over on her side.

"What'll I do?" Tiger complained. "Kennedy's moved up to Albuquerque."

"You mean you got nobody to connect with?" Ralph said. "I kept after you to get somebody onboard."

"Damn," Tiger said. "You can't win for losing. Where the hell am I going to find one to come out here? Even if I do, it'll cost a fucking fortune. Damned cat," he said. "Just when she was going to make some money for me."

"Get going," Ralph said. "You need somebody quick—if you can find anybody. I'll take care of her in the meantime." He offered her more water.

"That damn fool—I'll bet he never made any kind of contact

with a vet in the area. I asked him more than once. Just counting on some off-the-wall kind of luck, while doing everything to blast it." He went for a dart gun.

I could hardly stand it. Antoinette would lie still for a moment, then let out a howl and roll around some more.

When he came back with the gun, he waited for the right moment to send the dart. It hit her and she jerked and howled. "She'll be quiet soon."

"What's the matter with her?" I tried to keep from crying.

"I don't know, sweetie. Food poisoning maybe, though cats usually don't eat tainted food. Maybe something else. If Tiger made some kind of mistake . . ."

"I think you better go on home," he said gently. "I'll take good care of her, you can bet on it."

I didn't want to leave. "There's nothing more to be done right now," he said in a voice that told me not to argue. "This'll quiet her down till we can get somebody here."

In the midst of things, Priam showed up. He'd come to have a word with Tiger about the rent and the lease, only Tiger had brushed him aside and gone off to phone.

"Come on," Priam said to me. "You're not going to do any good around here. Just be in the way." He'd have grabbed me if I hadn't pulled my elbow out of his reach. I had a sick feeling in the pit of my stomach. I couldn't keep from crying.

"Don't give me any of that," Priam said. "You got better things to cry about. If you don't, I'll think up a few."

I just ran on across the highway, bawling like crazy. Nobody had to tell me about the rest. I just stayed away. Tiger owed me four dollars, but I didn't try to collect. Every day I expected Angie Cummins or somebody official to come back and close up the place. The sign was still lit up—the jungle was still at your door. And every once in a while I'd see Tiger coming or going. I hoped to see Ralph, but somehow I missed him.

There was a little flurry of business around Labor Day weekend, and for a while the parking lot was full of cars. Tiger actually came over and paid me my four dollars and asked me if I'd help him out.

And Priam said, "Go on—you got nothing better to do," Somehow whatever I did never climbed the ladder of the worthwhile.

"I see you got a little business," he said to Tiger. "Just you don't lose sight of that rent money. I ought to be charging you interest."

I thought the animals were glad to see me, but when I looked into Antoinette's cage and saw that only Caruso was there, I just couldn't keep from crying.

"She'll be all right," Tiger said, "Had to do a little surgery, but she'll be back good as new." I didn't believe a word of it.

"Come on now," he said, trying to brighten things up. "Can't have you scaring all the customers."

At that moment, four of them appeared. A car stopped and a family with two little girls got out. Ralph wasn't there yet, and I was wishing he'd turn up. The place felt really creepy—a lonesome feeling with a bad smell mixed in—and I didn't want to be there. But it was either that or nothing. The stink from the monkey cage was something awful. When I looked in, I could see only one of the gibbons, and then I spotted the female all curled up in the far corner, like she wasn't going to move. The male was screeching and leaping around where she was.

"Oh, look, he's swinging her around," one of the little girls said. "What's the matter with her? Is she sick?"

"Come on, Mary, Elizabeth." The mother said, hustling the two little girls away. "Daddy's waiting, and we need to move on."

The day slogged on like it was moving its wheels through a swamp. Ralph never showed up, and Tiger didn't come over to pay the rent. When Priam went over to the zoo around closing time, a Mexican fellow with only a little English told him that Señor Tigre was in town. Priam kept a lookout for him until suppertime, but there was no Señor Tigre.

Priam was not happy. "That lowdown, sneaking sonofabitch . . . After all I've done for him . . . These beans are terrible," he said as he poked at his supper.

"They came from the same can as the others."

"Don't you get smart with me," he snarled, "or I'll let you have it."

When Tiger did put in an appearance, much later that evening, he had a hangdog look and no cash. "That was a whopper of a vet bill," he said. "Put me way behind——." But now that he'd paid off his supplier and the vet, he'd be able to catch up. He'd pay next Thursday.

"I got to get me a tiger to breed," he said, then looked over at me as though he'd put his foot in it. "What I mean to say . . ." but Priam cut off his splutter.

"You pay me now or clear out," Priam said, coming at him from the nasty mood that had been building all day. "I'll get the sheriff onto you—just wait and see. He's a pal of mine. You got something underhanded going on, he'll catch up with you right quick."

"You'll have your money," Tiger insisted. "You'll get everything that's coming to you." He held out his paw for Priam to shake. "It's all between friends, that's what I say. I'll see what I can do at the bank. It might take a day or two."

"Friends!" Priam muttered as if it were a curse, as he watched Tiger take himself off. He said a few things for his own satisfaction, then took out the whiskey to rescue the evening, and turned on the TV. I kept out of his way. The hooch never sweetened the mix. Finally, he fell asleep right there at the kitchen table, his head leaning on his arms.

Sometime past midnight I woke up suddenly, as if I'd smelled smoke. When I looked out from where I was sleeping on the porch I could see lights, with men moving around behind them. I was in a good spot to see what was going on. From across the road, a clattering of metal and doors opening, and animals occasionally breaking into a bark or a howl. Nothing unusual about that. We'd hear animal noises most nights. They were pretty quiet considering. The night was clear and cloudless.

The big trailer that had come the first day, the great metal ark with all the animals, stood with its doors open, reflecting the lights from the flashlights as the men moved around. Tiger was there supervising the operation as they loaded up the animals. I couldn't make out if Ralph was there.

Tiger had some guts all right, thinking he'd pull it off. But he knew he could figure on a few things—whiskey and deep sleep for starters.

Priam was really out of it, snoring so loud he'd have slept through the Second Coming. I didn't know whether to wake him or let him be. But I figured it was my hide if I didn't give him the news, so I went in and tugged at his arm half-heartedly. No response. I tried once more, a little harder. "Lemme be," he sputtered, pushing away my hand, but he didn't wake up.

Oh well, I thought. *You told Tiger to pay up or clear out. You called the shots. And Tiger made a clear choice.* I couldn't exactly blame him.

When it came light, the wind was going at it full tilt, blowing scraps of paper and tumbleweeds through the lot just like it always did.

At first, Priam was too woozy to know what was going on. But around our place everybody was prepared, everybody except Priam. After I fed them, both the cat and dog hightailed it in their favorite directions. We didn't see Spot, who had only one little spot by his nose, for three days. And Sunset was on the highest branch of the box elder. They could read the signs.

I made coffee for Priam and waited for him to wake up and work into the day. All the while the explosion I was expecting just hung in the air gathering tindilization, as I called it. I was breathing down to my navel, trying to steady myself for when it hit.

I was glad the zoo was done with, but what about Ralph? What would I do without him?—he was my one real friend. Plus I was worried about what would become of the animals, and I was still grieving over Antoinette. There was nothing on the horizon and nothing to do now but mope around with a hole in my heart.

I wanted like anything to go back to school. I was twelve and had already missed three grades. When the new social worker came around, Priam pulled out his old story with a few variations. My mama had been sick but was now back on her feet, and I'd be leaving any day for Texas—soon as she got her car fixed. I'd be living with my ma and going to school there. "I want to go to school," I kept saying.

"You got enough to do right here," Priam said. "I don't aim to have those bureaucracy fools poking into my business."

The words still burned right through me, even as I stood there hearing him stretch and hawk and spit and head towards the toilet to take his first leak of the day. I just stood there witless when he came out and started fumbling his way into his clothes and then watched him search around for his shoes and swear when at first he couldn't find them and then sit down to work into them.

"What are you staring at?" he said. "Go out and feed the chickens."

"They been fed."

"Then cook me some eggs."

Before I knew what was happening, something burst inside me, and I started jumping up and down and hollering. "I want to go to school, I want to go to school." I don't know what hit me. "I want my mama." I yelled. I couldn't remember if I'd ever had one but I wanted her anyway.

He got up with one shoe on, gimped his way right quick to where I was jumping around and walloped me so hard on the side of the head, he sent me reeling.

"You pull that kind of shit on me and . . ." He would have grabbed me and done it again, but I kicked him in the shin and turned and ran so fast my legs felt electric and my feet hardly touched the ground. I knew he couldn't follow me, not where I was going—down to the arroyo over my secret path. A huge granddaddy of a prickly pear sat right on the way, and you had to be extra careful to get past because the rocks made it narrow there. Then under the barbed wire, down a little incline, and around a big patch of scrub cedar. He'd never get me there. Too many rocks along the way. Besides, he was going to have other things to think about.

I walked along the bed a ways to a flat rock where I liked to sit. I found me a stick to make lines in the sand. Sometimes I wrote my name over and over with printed letters and cursive, with capital letters and small ones. Grace. And I'd say it over and try to imagine what she was. The Grace I meant to be.

I was still all worked up. I couldn't catch my breath, and every once in a while I'd just let out a sob and shake all over. I took the rock off the top of the place where I'd stashed my money, added the four dollars Tiger had paid me and two I'd gotten my last workday, and counted it. I had twenty-eight dollars, but I didn't know where that would get me. After that I kept dreaming of places I could go someday—Albuquerque, New York, L.A., New Orleans, trying to taste their sounds and conjure them up. Whoever it was I'd made up for myself to be, I had to keep holding onto her skirt. Putting myself inside her so she wouldn't get away from me. She had to live something different, but I had no idea yet what it was. I just had to keep dreaming about her till I could make something happen.

III.

When I came back to the yard, there was an old gray Ford sitting there that didn't belong to anybody I knew. I walked around it, gave it the once over. It had a license plate that said Missouri, The Show Me State, a big dent in the back fender and a long scrape on the driver's side. Guess that showed a few things. Scattered on the seat inside were empty soda cups and plastic water bottles and a French fry carton and hamburger wrappers. In back was a blanket and a stuffed teddy and a seat for a little kid. I didn't know anybody in Missouri.

Suddenly I was aware the chickens were making an awful racket—like they did if there was a coyote or a weasel in the neighborhood. I let go of the car and hurried over to the shed. Sitting just to one side was the tank that had held the python. In front was a piece of cardboard with something written on it in black ink: "Well, Honey, here's a little present for you. Keep him fed and warm and he'll make you a good pet. So long and good luck in your life.

Love ya,

Your friend, Ralph."

I kept it under my pillow after that and have always kept it with me.

The heating pad was lying next to the tank. Only thing missing was the python, so I went searching for it. When I went in the direction of the shade, I found it stretched out with the head and body of a Rhode Island Red inside, bulging out its middle, feet and legs sticking out its jaw. He was still working on it. Probably the best meal it had had during its whole career.

Carefully, I gathered up the snake, put it back in the tank and closed it up. I was all in a quandary about what to do next. But I figured since we had company, I was safe for the time being. I went in the screen door, careful not to let it clatter behind me.

A woman was occupying Priam's chair, a big woman with some of her lapping over the edges. The first thing that came into my head was, "How's she gonna get out of there?" Her face was a moon, like a peach gone soft. And her makeup gave her cheeks a peach-like glow. You could tell she'd been really pretty once, before everything got heavy and saggy. She had fierce blonde hair sticking out around her head, like a dandelion gone to seed, and her lips were colored a red on the dark side, but still bright. She was wearing a white jersey and a blue skirt with yellow sun-bursts all over it. Jazzy. She had on earrings with silver hoops, and lots of bracelets on her arms. You could tell she liked to dress up. I liked all that too. She had style. The perfume she had on was a knock-over. It made a whole climate.

Something moved at the back of the chair. A little pale face leaned out just a bit and then drew back. I moved so I could see who it was. A little boy, just standing there, not making a sound, a kid maybe five or six, on the small side, tow-headed, with a face all screwed up at me like he'd as soon bite you as look at you. And then it just turned blank—nobody there. You could tell.

"Well, here she is," the woman said, like she'd been sitting there just waiting for me to show up. "Come give us a kiss, Sugar." She offered her arms. I stopped dead in my tracks.

"Lookit here," Priam said. "I don't want any trouble, you get me? You left—I took this brat, wherever she came from, and now you're coming back . . ."

"As if you didn't have anything to do with it, you old bag of guts." She pushed herself forward and hoisted herself up. She planted herself in front of Priam like she wasn't about to budge.

"Once I was young and could have had a life . . ."

"Don't give me any of your horse manure. Every male in the territory was in your pants. You were lucky to get what you got, considering that mother of yours."

"You don't know anything about it. You just want to make a case against me. As if Elsie didn't exist, God save her. As if you didn't know anything about that either. Well, she's gone, and I've got to start all over."

She turned to the boy. "This is your home now." Then looking to me—"Take care of him, Sweetheart." She was turning to go—Just like she'd dropped off a parcel.

I could hardly take it all in. Suddenly there were two creatures I was supposed to take care of besides the chickens. My head was spinning. And was this my mother? I couldn't feature it.

"Now you just wait a minute, Loosie Goosie," Priam said, putting his face in hers. "You pulled that trick on me once, and I'll be a cross-eyed monkey if you're gonna do it again. Haul ass and take what you came with."

"Nobody to stop me," she said. "From now on, I'm doing what I damn well please. Otherwise the cops'll be out here quicker than you can flip a dime. All I got to do is whistle," she said.

"Just you try," Priam said. "I got my connections, too." But it sounded pretty hollow to me. He stood glaring at the woman—was her name Lucy?—like he was trying to face her down. Then his eye went to the menace that swung back and forth on the corner of the chair. "I want you both out of here right this minute."

But she jutted out her chin and stood her ground, not about to knuckle under. I admired her moxy. "Well, you got some figuring to do." She turned towards the door. "Otherwise, there's going to be trouble. And I mean TROUBLE." Bam! And then a pause for it all to soak in. She even turned back and stamped her foot. "It's only what's owing to Elsie. It's your chickens come home to roost. You can add them to the lot in the yard," she said with a sour laugh. "Only they're scruffier than the ones you got out there."

I looked from one to the other, both in their separate hostilities. If it came to taking sides, I was between a rock and a hard place. And the Kid was paler than ever. But he didn't move or whimper—just stood like a stump.

Good grief! I thought. *Suppose he does wind up here? Worse luck for him.* I wanted to run off and disappear for the rest of the day. This was only part of the trouble, and the other part hadn't landed yet. What was operating here and what was waiting there made an interesting tension—two people ready to kill each other on the one hand, and on the other a python coiled up with a chicken in its gizzard. More excitement than in the average day. Interesting—if you had the stomach for it. But all that could wait. What I needed was to see the end of this installment so there'd be room enough for the next.

It looked like the Lucy person was winning. Priam was stalled, you could tell, but you never knew what the old weasel would come up with. "Look," he said, taking out his wallet. "If you're hurting for cash . . ."

He was actually going to pay her money! My eyes were glued to that wallet. It was thick with bills. How much would he let go of? was the big question.

She let out a whoop that set every part of her body jiggling. I thought she'd never quit laughing. Priam just stood there, his face going all colors, the wind knocked out of his sales pitch. But it was a dangerous moment. He wasn't one to be laughed at. I figured she'd better watch her step.

"I knew it," she said, gasping for breath. "Even ready to part with a little cash. He'll go that far. I thought he'd cut off an arm first." And her laughter went peeling out in all directions. "And how much will it take to pay me off?" She wasn't any more curious than I was.

"Look at him, will you." She was inviting me over to her side. It was okay by me till I remembered the python. That was still hanging fire and promised a fight maybe equal to this one.

The light was high on Priam's bald spot. He was ready to throw something in her face, punch her out. I knew that look. He held up the wallet. "Take it all, damn you. Take it and git."

"The soul of generosity. But I won't starve out an old man," she crooned. "I'm not half so mean as that." You could see she enjoyed laughing at him, just taking her pleasure. "What do you want?" It was a curse.

"Only what you owe—only you'll never be done paying. And don't get it in your head you can dump either one of the kids or do them any meanness. My eye will be on you. They've got places for people like you."

"Come on now, Babe . . ."

"There he is—" she said, like she was doing a demonstration. "Trying to honey me up. Like in the old days. I been through all that," she reminded him. "All the slick-tongued conniving you're so good at. He's not even human," she said, to the room or maybe to the whole world.

Then she did a straight shot to me. "And don't get it in your mind I'm your mother," she said. "I'm no kin and I don't owe you nothing. You were found in an alley, out with the trash. And if you're thinking I'm fat and ugly—all this bulk . . ." She gave a bitter laugh. "But that's what keeps them off me. And that's all I care about."

"Get out of here." Priam said, grabbing up a skillet. "Get out . . ."

"Think of that," she says. "First he won't let me go. Now he's trying to kill me." That picture made her laugh, too. "Just knock me down." She was tickled. "Then you can pick me up." She stood in place like a mountain. "I'll be leaving in my own sweet time," she drawled. "This one here needs to know a few of life's lessons before I go."

He had taken a step towards her, raising the skillet, but it looked like she had him. What would he do with her if she were laid out flat on the linoleum? And what would they do with him if he had to call for help?

"Nobody owns you," she went on. "You were just born, that's all. And so was he—the Kid. You don't belong to anybody—just remember that." Then to Priam: "And just remember what I told you—you take care of them, or else. There's an envelope they've got with some interesting facts inside. Like what you were up to back then and where you got a big wad of cash."

And she turned again and made her careful way out of the house. No need to hurry. "I'm free, damn you all," she threw back at us. "I'm free as a bird."

We all stood watching her go, not saying a word. I didn't dare look at Priam. Free as a bird. And where did that leave us? The Kid didn't make a move, and his face was still a blank. He was sucking his thumb. It was all too confusing—

Outside the car started up with a lot of noise and clatter like the whole engine was going to shake itself to pieces. It snickered down and died, then wheezed and coughed as she started it up again. If that jalopy was headed back to Missouri, it had a ways to go. But suddenly, with a whoom, the Ford shot off down the road, the dust thicker than a smoke screen behind it. Our visitor was gone, and the

Kid was there, a new part of the household. For a moment, there was a quiet like a hole in the middle of the day. Then slowly, it just closed up. Maybe none of it had really happened. Only when Priam went outside, the Kid's car seat was lying on the ground along with the blanket and the stuffed teddy.

That set him off. He came in and let go a blue streak that left the air crackling. Then he gave out with a side of an argument that had been lying in wait, but hadn't yet been delivered. "You'd think I was just a low-down skunk. She wants to dump all the blame on me. But let him tell you what she did, just making a fuss, having her way with everything. Blackmail, I tell you—you see what she did."

He'd really worked himself up, yelling and shaking his fist, spewing out all the things he'd been deprived the opportunity to throw into the pot before. As he told her off in several versions, and added a few other grudges, storming around the house as he carried on, he knocked over a lamp and got tangled in the cord. That took the breath out of him, and he staggered over to the armchair, so recently vacated, sank down and gasped. I handed him a glass of water. He took a pull, made a face like I'd tried to poison him and made me come take the glass. "I hate that stuff."

He always came on strong and then you got to watch him go limp. I was looking for a good moment to make him acquainted with the python. I felt something tickling inside my throat and I had to cover my mouth and pretend there was a cough coming.

He turned on me. "It's all your fault, damn you." I wanted to stick out my tongue but managed to keep my head.

"Well, don't just stand there. Pick that stuff up outside and stow it away somewhere. And that thing, too."

Next to the chair was a little scarred pink cardboard suitcase with a blue dog on the front. I went and picked it up.

With that, he gave his welcome to the Kid. "Well, Kid. Looks like we're stuck with you. If you piss your pants, you'll have to sleep out with the chickens."

He muttered a few things to himself, then his eyes roved around the room as though he was seeing it for the first time.

Where was he going to put the Kid?—that was the question. The cat and dog lived outside. The chickens had a shed at the side of the yard. The truck sat out in the drive. He had the only real bedroom. I slept on the porch in warm weather, on a pullout couch in the winter. He pulled himself up, went back to his room, and brought out a pile of old quilts and blankets. He folded up three or four, some for the top, some for the bottom, and put them on the floor under the window. "Guess you can sleep there," he said. It wasn't much of a bed, but it would have to do

"And you'll have to look out for him," he said to me, "and see he doesn't get into mischief."

I went up and tried to take the Kid by the hand, but he pulled away and hid his face in the chair. I knew I couldn't pick him up—he'd just start kicking and hitting—and I wasn't sure what to do. I didn't want him to throw himself into a fit.

"I got something to show you," I said, bending down so my face was on a level with his, but he turned away. "And I'll bet you never saw anything like it." I waited a moment. He didn't move.

"Do you want to see? I'll show you." I guess he went over it in his mind because he turned around, and I reached out my hand and touched his arm. He flinched a little, but he didn't pull away. I knew I had to get him to trust me, like Ralph had done with me and the snake—the way he treated all the animals. Finally, I led him outside.

Priam had settled himself in the big chair, with a *Playboy* magazine in his lap, ignoring us. The day had started out pretty hopping, like you'd missed a curve and gone sliding down the rocks to where a grizzly bear waited below. And the day wasn't over.

I took the Kid by the hand and led him round by the shed. There inside the tank, the python was still working on the chicken. I was wondering how he felt about the feet—they seemed pretty tough and indigestible to me.

"He doesn't have a name yet," I said. "Maybe we can come up with one."

I'd had a hard time trying to name the python. Ralph and I had gone over a few possibilities. For a week or so, I'd called him "King," but, though he was impressive, he wasn't twenty-five or thirty feet like the really big pythons. Ralph suggested "Dark Prince," and then with a laugh, "Deep Throat."

The Kid kept staring at the snake. I didn't know if he was scared or just fascinated. "It's a python," I told him. "It won't hurt you, but you have to be careful." I remembered what Ralph had told me.

I was going to have to get it into the house, bring it in like Lucy had done the Kid, working on a powerful argument so it wouldn't get chucked out. It would take some thinking. It's right cold at night in the desert, and if the snake caught pneumonia, that would be the end of it.

Back of the shed was an old wagon I'd sometimes played with or hauled wood in. I brought it up. It was hard working the tank up onto the wagon, but I got one end up and pushed up the rest. I had to pull the wagon slowly around the weeds and tree roots until we got it up to the house. I propped the door open, then shoved it up the porch step to bring it inside. I figured it wasn't going to get any better welcome than the Kid, but once I'd got the thing inside, we'd go on from there.

Priam looked up. "What the hell's going on?"

"It's a python," I told him straight out.

"A python?" I thought he'd fall over getting out of the chair. "Why that son-of-a-bitchin' viper! Leaving me with that critter instead of the rent money. His idea of a joke, I'll bet. I wish he'd come back so I could punch him in the Adam's apple. Even if the skin is worth something . . ."

I almost panicked. The moment was full of peril, but just then I was struck by an idea. "That snake's worth far more alive," I said. "It's worth lots. Maybe Tiger was trying to do well by you. Seeing as how he couldn't pay, he's left you something valuable."

"How do you know so much?"

"Ralph told me. He said it would grow to be thirty feet, and then it would make a piece of change like you wouldn't believe." One thing was leading to another. Amazing how inventive you can get when you're in a tight corner. And I'd been learning a few things from

Priam himself, about pumping up your product, just giving it all you got, even if it was a bald-faced lie. I didn't know if he would swallow my line, but I had to bet on it.

"He said that? You're not shittin' me, are you?"

"That's what he said."

He was looking at me slit-eyed, trying to figure out if I was lying, but I was holding my face steady even though my heart was thumping like a trapped animal's. Carpet pythons don't get all that big, only four to six feet. But I knew he wouldn't be impressed with some little midget snake. On account of me, the snake would either live or die—I was holding out for the snake. I'd learned something about taking sides. It wasn't going to be easy. To slip past the old reptile standing there, I'd have to be part snake myself and part tiger as well, and canny as a fox.

I could see he was going back and forth in his mind. It didn't take any genius. The idea of having a snake around was giving him the fidgets. "It would have to go out in the shed," he said.

"No, it can't. It gets cold out there, and the chickens aren't about to keep it warm—(There was one less to worry about). This is the heating pad they used in the zoo. It goes under the tank."

He still didn't catch on. I'd given him the hint. Only he wasn't connecting. Or maybe he was just resisting. I let it sit with him. I could tell he was nervous just having to look at the python, but he hadn't let go of the idea it was worth big bucks. The snake lay there full of food and peaceful.

I went back to the money angle. "This one's real young," I said.

"How long does it take to get full grown?"

"Depends," I said. "I haven't seen one reach its growth, but I'll bet they jump right along. There are lots of zoos waiting to get their hands on one. And all those outfits making snakeskin purses. Then they're worth real money—that's what Ralph said."

"But how're we gonna keep it? How do you know it won't get out and bite you or strangle you or me or him," he said, the first sign that now the Kid was part of our domestic arrangements. "I heard some little toddler got mangled down in Florida."

"That was an alligator," I said. "They're dangerous creatures. Two big rows of razor-sharp teeth. This one won't hurt you if he's well fed. Not a tooth in his head. Ralph told me about handling snakes."

"So you think you got it in you?" Priam said. "I sure as hell don't want to mess with it."

Didn't figure you did, I thought.

"How about just killing it and we'd be shut of it," he said.

He was actually willing to let go of the profits. It was harder than I thought.

"Well," I said, "if you want to throw away hundreds of dollars. We've got a real opportunity come our way, and I'll take care of it. You'll see."

He thought it over. "I don't like the color of it. I don't like things that crawl. The whole idea gives me the weemies."

"It'll keep the mice down, earn its keep."

"I just wish that damned cat would hold up her end."

"Well the python will more than make up for her and get its own dinner into the bargain. I'll just let him crawl around every once in a while—when you're not here. Get its dinner. Zap—and there's a mouse gone. And hundreds of dollars waiting for you."

He shrugged and sighed and wiped his hand across his forehead. Maybe I was wearing him down. It had been a pretty tough day so far. "Okay, okay,' he said, "it's your baby, but if there's any trouble . . ."

"Won't be." A brand new idea hit me. "Only I got to learn some things. I want a library card of my own and books to read. I got to know some more about pythons. And I need a bicycle to ride so I can get to town and back on my own."

"Getting pretty fancy there, aren't you? A bicycle. How about spending some of that money you got this summer?"

"No," I said. "You're going to get big money for that snake, and you already got part of mine. If you want me to take care of him . . ." I pointed to the Kid.

"Damn," he said, wiping his forehead again. "I need a snort of whiskey."

I waited.

"Only you got to do all the work. And the boy and the chickens."

It was as good a bargain as I was likely to get.

I was in motion right after lunch, the right moment to be off the precincts while Priam took in what the rest of the day had to offer. Three miles, but it hardly seemed like one. I skipped over the distance. I was going to have wheels and as many books as I could carry. I felt like I'd grown wings. The bike would have to have a basket.

I wanted a blue one, royal blue. The bicycle I ended up with was a used girl's bike, not quite as old as creation, with dull green fenders and a basket. Ed Forster, who owned the bike shop, put a new chain on it and replaced the tires. It worked good as new. I got a library card and checked out a good book on snakes and a book about dogs. And some books for the Kid. I had gotten my way, this time at least. And though Priam must have guessed that I knew all about Tiger taking off before he did, he didn't start in on me. Maybe he'd had enough for one day.

IV.

"Once upon a time there was a snake—a little snake, nothing much, just crawling on the ground. Nothing else. Just the snake."

"That's all? Where did it come from?"

"From the dirt—it was living in a tunnel and one day it saw there was light outside and just poked up and came on out."

We were sitting on some rocks not far from the arroyo. The python was lying in the grass a little way off ready to seize its chance for supper. Dining at the Prairie Dog Colony Café, not far off. He would lie there quietly waiting till one of the dogs poked up a head to take in the day, and then he'd let go, zap it with his tongue and unhinge its jaw. Or else he'd slip into a hole and take his prey. Sometimes he'd snare a young rabbit. When we were ready to go home, I'd gather him up and put him around my shoulders like a scarf and off we'd go. He was doing well, that snake.

The Kid liked coming down with me to my special place. He thought the snake was pretty keen too. Sometimes we were there for hours, keeping out of Priam's hair. For a long time, I couldn't get the Kid to talk. I was sure he knew how, only he held back. But then I started telling him stories, some from the books I got from the library and others I made up in my head. I'd take home storybooks that had pictures in them. He liked the pictures. And I bought some crayons for him and a notebook with blank paper. But he didn't use them, not then. Not even a coloring book. It was stories he wanted. And if I paused and didn't go on, he'd give me a little nudge.

"And what did it see?"

"Nothing to see. Just distance. No matter how much you kept looking. Just distance ahead of you and distance behind, and more distance all around and up and down. Pretty dull—no colors in it. Not like here. You got all these rocks and cactus and grass and Indian paintbrushes."

"Nothing at all? Didn't it have a mother or father?"

"Nope, nobody down there." The Kid thought about that and clammed up for a while. He picked up a rock and threw it at a mocking bird sitting up on a branch not far from us. The bird flew off just in time. The Kid had a good aim. "I don't like this story."

"But what do you guess it did?"

"I dunno." He'd gone sullen. I was used to that. I looked to where the python had been. It had crawled a little farther on, had got its dinner pretty well taken care of. We'd wait till it got it settled inside.

"The snake looked around and said, 'Well, this sure isn't anything to brag about. It's cold out here, and it'll freeze my innards if I don't keep moving. And I'm tired of crawling on my belly'"

"It had to hatch something good. Took a while. First it grew feathers all over its body because of the cold wind blowing. And pretty soon it had some extra. They started pooching out into these shapes . . ." I reached out with my arms curved and my fingers spread out. "What d'you know, he had wings."

The Kid couldn't believe it. "Just like a bird?"

"That's right. Took him a while to figure out what they were for. But he flapped them up and down. Pretty neat. And after he lifted up and flopped down a time or two, he lifted up and there he was—flying."

The Kid got up and flapped his arms. "I'm a bird," he yelled and ran past the trees and up the hill. "I'm a bird, and I can fly," he cried out as he came pelting down.

When he settled back down and got his breath, he said. "What was the snake's name?"

I hadn't made it that far. "Well, it wasn't just a snake any longer—it could fly."

"A bird and a snake?' The Kid laughed. "That's funny."

"It was a special snake." I had to search around a bit. "Its name was Pajarito. Little Bird—." It just came to me.

"What happened then?"

I could see where the sun was. "I'll tell you next time. There's nothing in the house to eat and I've got to ride into town and get us some hamburger for supper."

It was up to me. The truck was broken down, as usual, sitting there in the shop waiting for the parts to come in. Seems like the old thing had broken down so many times every part had been replaced, usually with other old parts that had already seen wear and tear. Now it took some kind of genius to fix it. My bicycle came in pretty handy.

I picked up the python and put him around my shoulders, and we left the arroyo. I didn't know much about cooking, but I got us fed. I could heat things up from a can and cook eggs and macaroni and cheese and fry potatoes and make pancakes from the Aunt Jemima box and cook hamburgers and even pork chops.

"About time you showed up," Priam said when we got home.

I put the python—now Pajarito—back into the tank.

"Now get done with that snake." Priam said, "I can hear my gut growling."

Priam never came near the snake. You could tell he still wasn't thrilled about having it for company. Sometimes when it stirred, he'd give a start, and when I took it up and put it around my shoulders, he squinched up his face like there was a bad smell in the house. If there was, it likely came from him because he thought water was bad for you and didn't wash much. The snake was much cleaner. Sometimes I'd take it out in the yard when there was a big enough puddle for it to bathe in, or else, when there was a pool in the bottom of the arroyo after the rain had gone.

Priam was waiting for the day to arrive when the snake was big enough to turn into a pile of cash. It did grow a few inches, but naturally, I didn't tell him it was as big as it was going to get.

So the days went skipping by, me taking care of the chickens, the snake, and the Kid, Priam just laying around—putting his mind to important things, or so he said. He had his "disability," he'd managed to wangle somehow, and every month he sent me to the Post Office to collect an envelope from Social Security.

I think he just forgot about us, even the python, so long as we went our own ways and didn't pester him, so long as there was food on the table and whiskey in the bottle to help pass the long nights. We just kept on living, and time kept sucking the present into the past.

The Kid didn't know when his birthday was, but I figured he must be at least six. I was trying to teach him how to read, and he was picking it up pretty quick and was proud when he could sound out words he didn't know. He liked saying them over to himself until they belonged to him, allowed him to put himself inside them. He liked to reel off big words even if he didn't quite know what they meant.

He still wanted me to tell him stories, even though he was beginning to read some on his own. Once I started with Pajarito, he had to have a story every chance we got. It kept me going, a real challenge, trying to come up with new adventures.

Something had been set in motion, I realize now, and it was amazing to me how the story kept opening out as we went along. I made that discovery one bright afternoon after rain kept us inside for a couple of days.

We went down to the arroyo to our special rocks, and I set down Pajarito to laze in the grass. He'd had enough food to make him sluggish. He wasn't going anywhere.

I was enjoying the sun myself, as I sat there with the Kid beside me, trying to work my brain into a new part of the story.

"Well, once he had wings, he was a different creature altogether. They definitely changed him." As soon as I said that, things started coming to me. "He was going to tackle the distance."

I looked at the Kid, and his eyes were bright with excitement. "A fear voice rose up inside him and said, Stay here. You'll lose your way and sink into the distance forever."

I turned to the Kid again. "What do you think he did?"

"HE FLEW INTO THE DISTANCE," the Kid announced, leaping up and shouting into the air.

"Yes indeed. He flew into the distance straight as an arrow. Flew till it made him dizzy—wasn't even a tree to land on." The Kid had settled down, was still with me, but I was getting lost in the distance myself and needed a little help. "He was so tired, he was afraid he was going to fall out of the sky. When he looked down, it was like there was no bottom anywhere. He kept circling around, not knowing what to do. Just when he was about to give up—*I was just about in the same place storywise*—he thought he saw something below. He swooped down and what do you think he saw?" I waited.

"Water!" the Kid yelled, leaping up again.

"That's it—that's exactly what he found. And what did he do then—take a bath?"

"No," the Kid said, with disgust. "He made mud."

"Of course, he did."

It was a discovery—I had to hand it to the Kid. I didn't know how Earth got there, but things do happen without your knowing. It was a great discovery, not only for Pajarito, because you can make things out of mud.

There was a clay bank on the side of the arroyo, so we got some of it and began to make things. We made some fish to swim in the water, then birds to take off from the land. Big birds and little birds. Snake birds and bird birds. Trees were harder. In the story they just grew. But we did get a couple to stand up and keep their branches on. We made a dog and a cat. We made a line of trees on a big slab of rock. Then we put the birds all around them. It was getting on to late afternoon. "Hey, we'd better be getting on home." I got Pajarito and draped him around my shoulders.

The Kid was full of excitement about what we'd done. He wanted more animals, some wild ones, so I got some books with pictures of wild animals, like the ones in the zoo. Many afternoons later, we had a whole menagerie: rocks full of tigers and lions, elephants, monkeys and bears. The Kid wanted to fill a whole world full of animals. We let them bake in the sun. Only, a couple of days later, a real cloudburst pelted down, and when we came back, all our work had been washed down into little piles of mud. The Kid started to wail.

"We can make lots more," I said, "even better ones. We've got the knack."

That inspired the Kid to get out the crayons and the notebook I'd bought him, and he started drawing pictures of Pajarito and some of the animals he was going to make. I stuck some of the pictures up on the wall right over where he slept. I asked the Kid if he wanted to make any people. He shook his head no.

But he went to work on another figure out of clay. He kept hunched over it, not showing it to me, working at it quite a while till he got the face the way he wanted it and shaped the eyes and nose and mouth with stones he set into the clay. It was bigger than any of the other figures. When he was all done, it had a high forehead with rounded cheeks and a jaw that curved down from around the mouth and big eyes and a pointy nose and a mouth open like it was laughing.

"Who's that?"

"He likes to tell funny things," the Kid said. He wanted to carry it home and put it near the box elder tree in a place where Priam wouldn't see it. But then he changed his mind. We managed to find a good spot for it where it was sheltered from the rain and could look down on what we were doing and give us good ideas.

Sometimes after that, I'd find him sitting under the box elder tree when Priam wasn't there, telling stories to himself. He was always coming up with something inventive I hadn't seen or thought of before. I couldn't remember being a kid like that. There was nobody around except me to tell his stories to right then. No one else to talk to.

The Kid wanted a bird, now that Pajarito had turned into one, and a chicken wouldn't do. It couldn't get off the ground; the one he wanted had to fly. I sometimes wondered if the Kid thought a bird might teach him how to do it himself. Maybe from the box elder, where he spent a lot of time looking out over the world, as if he might just take off into some other landscape. It was like he had only one foot on the ground and was making up his own story as he went along. Pajarito had made a powerful impression on him, more real than anything, except maybe the snake itself. He had a kind of wonder that the stories must have excited, and when I told him stories, we'd both get so caught up in them we forgot where we were.

So now he had to have a bird. It wasn't enough just to make one up. I'd noticed a couple of ravens in a tree at the edge of a shelf of rock up the hill past the arroyo, I figured they had a nest there, given the time they spent winging back and forth. Thought I might climb up and steal one of the young, if I could manage it. I was good at climbing. I waited till I saw the parents fly off and made it up the hill to where it grew steep. There were footholds where I could climb, and sure enough, there was a nest with little ones in it, just about to the stage where they could fly. They made quite a racket when they saw me. I quick grabbed one by the feet before the parents got back and swooped down on me, was on the ground in a jiffy with only a skinned elbow and knee. I put the raven in my jacket pocket and zipped the pocket to where the bird could still breathe without getting away. It took me quite a while to get back down from the rocks with that bird struggling against me. But finally, it quieted down.

A raven. The Kid looked at me like I was the fairy godmother, and I was pretty excited by my little escapade. The Kid had his bird, just the right color for a black snake to turn into, with a nice purplish sheen and a yellow bill for just the right touch. We got a box from the grocery store and a piece of screen from the shed to put over and protect it from the cat, and made a nest inside with grass and twigs. I bought some bird feed with grain and seeds in it and told the Kid it would like insects if he wanted to catch some. It was his bird, so I left it to him to take care of. Pretty soon, it was riding around on his shoulder, and they had a language of sounds to exchange with each other, bird-boy talk. I got pretty friendly with it myself.

The raven became Pajarito, too. When I asked the Kid about the snake, he said that was also its name. He had no problem with that—he was a snake before he became a bird.

The Kid was my shadow. He'd help me pick up the place and feed the chickens and even dry the dishes. We finally got him a little cot he could sleep on and some toys and clothes from the St. Vincent de Paul's. He was growing, and he didn't look so pale as when he first came. To me, he could talk a blue streak. For a while, another Mexican family turned up and moved into the haunted shack. Just squatted there. Priam told them they could stay if they cleaned up the whole place. When he wasn't helping out, a boy named Pablo came over to play. At first, the Kid just hung behind me, but Pablo had a football, and he'd kick it across the yard and pound over after it. Then the Kid wanted to kick it too. Soon they were taking turns. After that, he'd go off and play with Pablo and his brother, Reynaldo. The Kid got to where he could talk Spanish with them, and they galloped around, yelling and shooting and playing cowboy games and doing other kid stuff. But suddenly, one day they were gone, and nobody knew where they went.

"Illegals," Priam said. "Should have turned them in." Maybe he even threatened to do it. Sent them moving on to find work or get to where they felt safe. We were back where we were before.

It was somewhere around that time I started roaming—now that I had the bicycle, I had a means of transportation. After I fed the chickens, cleaned out the snake tank, got food on the table and Priam and the Kid out of the way, I figured what I did was my own business. I'd ride my bike into town right after supper and sometimes I'd treat myself to an ice cream cone or go to the library on the evening it was open late and look at magazines or wander among the bookshelves. Sometimes I'd get a Nancy Drew mystery to read, or a teen book, but I tried other things, too.

I really loved going to the library. Mrs. Clayton, the librarian, took an interest in me and showed me books I might want to read. I read *Heidi* and *Anne of Green Gables* and *Black Beauty*. Once I got hold of a book called *Candide*, which was about the most far-out set of adventures anybody could come up with. Things always going from bad to worse. Almost worse than at our place. I couldn't even think of trying to make a garden in it with so many cactus thorns and brambles and other wicked stuff. And I hoped never to have to make a meal out of somebody's buttock to stay alive.

Priam left me pretty much alone, and the Kid had his own world. I suspect that, in Priam's mind, we belonged in the same department as snakes and ravens—critters you didn't want to meddle with if you could help it. As long as we weren't pestering him or costing him any real money, and I got my chores done, we didn't have to answer for much. That was my freedom, wandering off downtown and going to the library.

Besides, Priam lived in a beehive of distractions, his mind always somewhere else. He'd just keep scratching out numbers and notes on pieces of paper that I couldn't make head or tail of, his handwriting was so snaggled and ran slanting down the page. Sometimes it was telephone numbers or figures. But who or what they referred to was a mystery. He was in and out, busy all the time. And when he was sitting quiet, he'd get a look on his face I'd come to recognize. He'd be sitting in his chair, or at the kitchen table, his thumb and forefinger to his chin, and his eyes would go glassy. He wasn't seeing anything but what was in his head. He had a scheme growing, I could tell, and he was trying to nudge it along. The land across the highway was just sitting there empty, gathering tumbleweeds, and he had enough scheming in him to fill it right up.

But finally, it was my roaming that made Priam start noticing me. He didn't like it and he gave me stern warnings about where I could go and told me to keep off dark streets and avoid alleys. He needn't have worried. Mostly, if I didn't go to the library, I'd head straight for the Confectionery. The Kid wanted to go, too, and I couldn't put him off. Every once in a while, I'd let him ride on the back of the bicycle and go with me. Then I'd treat him to an ice cream cone—his favorite was chocolate—and we'd walk around and look in the store windows. When I went by myself, I'd hang around the magazine rack and read magazines till I got a frown from Cookie behind the counter. When he wasn't doing ice cream cones or waiting on a customer, he was keeping an eye out for the ones who read magazines without buying one.

But I think now that what really bothered Priam was that I was practicing up to push off on my own. I was seeing things and wanting things he didn't even know about. He couldn't keep tabs on me. It was what I was learning about freedom, though I hardly knew what the word meant. I guess the main thing I was waiting for was to grow up enough so I could get away. Only there was the Kid, and I didn't know what to do about him.

V.

One evening in the spring, when I was about to enter the Confectionery for a chocolate ice cream cone I'd been hankering for, I was stopped dead in my tracks by a poster in the window: a man and a woman caught in mid-air—her all glittery in blue and him in a white shirt and tights, reaching towards one another with arms outstretched. Glory! A circus was coming—right here to our spot in the road. I'd never been to a circus, but I'd listened to enough of Ralph's stories to know I had to see one. I had to watch that man and woman catch hold and swing into the next wonderful wide-open moment. A clown stood at the side, cheeks pooching out with his grin, a wink to his eye, his whole body telling you he knew something oh-so-special he couldn't keep it to himself. You had to be there so the secret could be yours.

It was my roaming that put me in the way of it, a whole new wonder. Oh, the discovery worked on me all right. I love a secret—I still love the sense that the next moment can give you an opening. A circus—not just pictures but the real thing. A current ran through my body. I was on fire, just aching to go.

"There's a circus come to town," I announced to Priam the moment I got home. "Right here—can we go? I just got to see it."

"Whatever for? Just a bunch of people swinging through the air like they didn't have the sense God gave a grasshopper, and animals jumping through hoops. Even a self-respecting dog knows better than to give over to that kind of nonsense."

I saw I'd gone the wrong way with it and could have kicked myself. I'd hit into his mean streak head-on. He liked to break the bubble, squelch the thing you'd been dreaming on—just for the satisfaction of seeing the wind drop from your sails. I kept on pleading and nagging, but he wouldn't budge.

"They're gyp joints," he said. "Just like taking your money and throwing it down a rat hole. You don't understand the bidness side of things." The way he said it you knew it was the kind of thing only somebody like him would be doing, and you'd never want to sticky up your fingers with it.

Finally I clammed up. No point fouling up the air with any more tindilization. Too much bad feeling in it already. I moped around for a while. But I wasn't going to give up. When I got the chance the next afternoon, I sneaked off and rode my bike into town and out to the fairgrounds to watch the tents going up. It was thrilling to watch the heaps on the ground being pulled up and turned into a great canvas castle. The beautiful red and white stripes of the tents and awnings took my breath away. I loved the little red and white flags waving.

I wanted like everything to buy a ticket. I'd have spent my last cent on one, I wanted to see the show that bad. Trouble was, I'd spent down my money buying the Kid and me things we wanted, like going to the movies and treats or toys when we went to town. Plus, I bought a pair of new jeans for myself. I had hardly anything left.

Sometimes I could fish out change from under the cushions in the big chair, if any of it dropped out of Priam's pockets. When I was little, he made me give it back. But now I never told him if I found any money. And when I had to go for groceries, I'd make him let me keep the change. Once I'd found a ten-dollar bill that had blown off into the weeds near the grocery store—a piece of luck. And I kept an eye peeled for change that had fallen near the parking meters. Every once in a while, I'd find a nickel or a dime that had rolled over the curb into the mud. I wished I had enough now for two tickets. If I went to the circus, the Kid would have to go, too. Otherwise it would be too cruel for me to go alone. I couldn't have kept from telling him about it. We were close. I had the feeling he understood way beyond what he gave out.

When I got out to the fairgrounds, I started poking around for a place where we could sneak in, like where the generators and power lines snaked along the ground. But there was a wire fence around them, and big signs that said Danger! Keep out! I walked around the back of the tent. But it looked like all the flaps were pegged down tight, hardly enough space for a cat to crawl under. I just wandered around, completely down at the mouth.

"Hello there, honey—you looking for somebody?"

Beside one of the trailers, a fellow sat in front of a mirror at a little table, applying makeup. His face had already been painted out, white as chalk, and he was putting large red spots on his cheeks. I stopped to watch.

"No," I said, "just looking around." But the sight of him brightened me immediately.

"You coming to see the matinee tomorrow?"

"I wish."

"You'll have to tell your mama and daddy to bring you."

He added heavy dark eyebrows and raised and lowered them as he gave me a cockeyed look. Then he started painting his mouth; only he didn't stop there. He painted all around his lips until his mouth came nearly as wide as his cheeks. Then he covered his head with a big reddish-orange mop of a wig.

"What do you think of that?" he said, showing me his face all made up. I had to grin.

"That's better," he said. "You were looking so far down in the mouth, the glum-warts were sprouting hairs."

"Glum-warts?"

"Oh, yeah. I've seen many a case of the miserables—you wouldn't believe. No cure like a circus—Hi de ho." He stepped up and did a little soft shoe bit.

"I've never been to a circus," I said. "And you're . . ."

"Ragamuffin, the clown," he said, as he stood there in his baggy pants, then pulled off his wig and made a low bow. "Beyond compare." Suddenly, he looked in horror at the mop of hair in his hand, felt around his bald head—covered with some skin-colored rubbery stuff—and slapped the wig back on his head. It hung lopsided over his ear. When I laughed, he tried to switch it around, but no matter what he did, it was off to one side, even over his eyes. I couldn't stop laughing.

"That's why I'm called Ragamuffin," he said, "Rags for short."

I didn't tell him mine. My name still seemed like the wig he'd just pulled off.

56

"Only now I got to get ready. In just about fifteen minutes, when the kids are out of school—you're here early, aren't you?—they're going to hold the traffic for us. And I'm going to ride down the street on Marshmallow over there, to let them know what thrills are waiting for them at the matinee tomorrow."

He pointed to where a little burro was tethered towards the back of his trailer. "One ass riding another," he said in a low voice. "Here I can be my natural self."

"Oh," I said, "she's beautiful."

We walked over to where she stood, and I rubbed her ears. He took a piece of sugar out of his pocket and let me feed it to her. Her nose tickled my hand. Then he held up a finger, opened up his mouth in a big O, as though he'd been hit by a brick, and said, "How would you like to ride her? She's a good girl. You'll be part of the publicity. You can wave to all your friends."

Not that I could count on any, but that didn't matter. He saddled her up, helped me mount, then took hold of the reins, and led us to one side. We stood waiting, while some of the other performers gathered. I recognized the trapeze artists I had seen on the poster. Seemed like they didn't belong on the ground.

A large man with a black top hat, a long-tailed coat, and a vest of gray patterned silk, ordering this one here and that one there, got the performers all lined up.

I was ready to burst with pride to be among them. We marched down the dirt road until we came to the intersection with the main street. The other intersections were cordoned off. First up was the elephant to lead the parade with a woman in a silvery top, short skirt, and tights seated on her curled trunk, blue plumes in a tall headdress. She was waving to the crowd that lined the street and blowing kisses. Three horses, sleek black, one white as shoe polish, and a high-stepping grey like I'd never seen before trotted behind her with their riders. Another clown, surrounded by dogs leaping down and back, leaned out of a little car he hardly fit in, horn tooting every second. And then Rags in front and me on the burro, waving to everybody like I was part of the circus too. There were kids I knew only by sight, and they looked pretty impressed. I felt I belonged with the circus.

"How about that," Rags said when we got back. "You're a real trooper."

I got to shake hands with Melba, the elephant woman, who wasn't all that young. But she'd uncoiled her red-blonde hair and let it out. Beautiful with the sun on it. One of the horsemen came up and grabbed a handful.

"Nice dye job," he said, and leapt back out of the way when she tried to slap him. He just laughed and said, "You make a great redhead."

A woman I hadn't noticed before came out of her trailer lugging a wicker basket, and when she set it on the ground and took off the lid, a python crawled up over the edge and onto the ground. It just kept coming, bigger than mine. That basket must have been heavy all right. Then she invited it up her leg and pretty soon she was wearing it around her middle, and then to her shoulders.

"I've got a python at home," I told her. "Only he's not nearly so big."

"No kidding," she said. "Well, aren't you the one?" Her name was Jessie, and she was tall and broad in the shoulders and she stood in the space like it was her property, and nobody better mess with her or tell her any different. But I was paying more attention to the snake.

"This is a good snake—tame," she said, "lets me do just about anything I want with it."

It was a lighter color than mine, more on the yellow side. I was dying to let it crawl around my shoulders, but Jessie said, "This thing weighs a ton." In a low voice, she said to Rags, "If she were a little older, I could teach her a few moves."

"That's for sure." He frowned, but she just laughed.

I could tell she wanted to tease him. "I wish I could be in the circus," I said.

She looked at me. "Well, it's a great life if you don't weaken. You gotta hang tough, that's all."

She got the snake all packed up in her basket and went off with a swing to her hips.

Rags had sat down at the little table, this time putting cream on his face and wiping off the makeup with a cloth.

"It's a hard life—What did you say your name was? Grace, eh?" when I told him. "Well, you need some of that in this life. Yes indeed, all you can get. On the road all the time. Performing afternoon and evening—Traveling for hours and to land in some little spot in the boonie lucky to have a post office. Land there all worn out, with a show to do right away. Eating on the run—food to make your stomach belch. Flopping down to grab a little shut-eye before the next round. You work so hard, you're beyond tired. And you'll never make it rich."

"But . . ." I was ready to protest anyway. It just seemed like all this was better than anything I knew: the days just stretching out one after the other and nothing in sight. Just distance—something to get lost in. "You get to see new things," I suggested.

"If they're worth seeing. But even they get old. Everything gets old." His face seemed creased into the oldness he was talking about. A cloud hung over us.

"And you make people happy."

He looked at me. "Yes," he said slowly. "One of the tricks of the trade. Till all the makeup comes off."

His makeup was off, and he was sitting there, a small man with freckles and sandy hair thinning from back of his forehead. I wanted the clown back. I couldn't bear what he was saying, I was so full of dreaming and longing.

"But don't listen to me," he said, giving me a big smile. "Just let's have one of those moments . . ." And like that, he was out from under the cloud. "Yes, indeed." He threw down the towel he'd used to dry his face, got up, and went inside his trailer. When he was back, standing in front of me, he made me close my eyes and hold out my hand. When I opened them, there were two tickets in my palm. I couldn't believe it. Before I could stammer a thanks, he pulled out three crumpled dollar bills and put those in my other hand. "You'll need some treats."

I was ready to bust. We were going to the circus, the Kid and I. "Let Priam try to stop us."

"See you tomorrow," he said. "Have a blast."

VI.

I left Rags with the precious tickets in my pocket, my head in a whirl. I was walking in a dream, dreaming of what the matinee would be like. Hardly noticing anything as I walked my bike around towards the other side of the trailer. Then something caught me—a voice, a laugh, and a hacking cough. I couldn't believe it. But here it came again. I stood stock still, listening with ears like they'd grown forward on stems. It had to be him, but how could it be? Goose bumps popped up all down my arms.

Priam! What was he doing there? Had he tracked me down? I laid my bike down on the ground and crept back to where he wouldn't see me. He was standing talking to Jessie and some other woman who had her back to me. It didn't look like Melba, who'd led the parade. Priam had his arm around her, whoever she was. I couldn't make out what they were saying.

When I got home I found a note from Priam. He had business in town and wouldn't be home till late. I'd have to get supper for me and the Kid—as if I didn't do that all the time anyway. Yard and house were empty except for Spot working on a bone near Priam's rocking chair. A few flies wheeling around for company. The usual, but with a blessed quiet. The afternoon was lazing towards evening. I called the Kid but got no answer. Figured he'd gone down to the arroyo, and that's where I found him, with the raven for company. It was almost like the two of them came together as one person, the bird almost always on his shoulder. The Kid was all absorbed—working hard making more figures out of the clay he was digging from the bank. He kept his creations under a shelf of rock with a piece of tin in front so the rain wouldn't get them, though sometimes they got pretty damp and had to be baked in the sun again.

I'd bought him some paints so he could decorate them after they got dry and hard. They looked pretty snazzy by the time he got done with them. He'd just finished painting one with a lean face and eyes turned in towards his nose. His name, he told me, was Spin with the Wind. Painted with yellow and blue stripes across the chest, a red body, and black hair in zigzags. "He's like this," the Kid said, holding out his arms and spinning himself around until he staggered over and collapsed in a heap, the raven having escaped up into the air. Then he leaped up and shouted, "Now he's READY."

He was all set to launch into a story he'd been hatching, only I stopped him. I was too excited for patience—I had bigger news. "We're going to the circus."

"What's that?" he said, kicking at a rock. I could tell he was pissed at me; I'd one-upped him. He'd been done out of his story. I just couldn't help it.

"There's an elephant and clowns and people standing on each other's shoulders and a gal who has the biggest python ever. All kinds of things. And funny dogs and maybe even a tiger." I hadn't seen one, but who knows, they maybe had one. I didn't tell him about the trapeze act and seeing people flying through the air. He'd have to see that without my taking away the surprise. "All in bright colors like you've been painting."

He thought it over as he kicked at a rock. "Where they coming from? And how do you know?"

"I been out to the fairgrounds and seen them with my own eyes. And everybody'll be there tomorrow."

"Wow," he said. "Wow." Then I took his hands and we both danced a little jig.

Next day when I told Priam, he was prickly about it. "Where'd you get the money for tickets?" he demanded. "You haven't been thieving off me, have you?"

"I got free tickets. A clown gave them to me."

"You'd better have sold 'em and taken the money. Give them over."

"No," I said. "I'll turn the python loose first, and I won't feed the chickens, and the Kid's gonna howl because I promised him. You want to listen to him howl? And I'll howl, too. We want to see the circus—and that's what we're going to do."

It wasn't any skin off his neck. Wasn't going to cost him a dime.

Except for the times I took the Kid to the library or to the movies or the swings in the schoolyard, we never went anywhere this special.

I didn't know what he'd do, so I just stood there, fire coming out of my eyes. I knew I could dodge out of his way and run if he tried to grab me. There was always the arroyo.

"Damn it, I got business to do." He looked at his watch. "Get outta my sight. Just this goddamn minute. If I didn't have to get on to town, I'd whale the tar out of you."

I don't know if he meant it—was maybe just giving us a hard time out of pure meanness. You could never predict what he'd do. But this time we took off like wild dogs before he found some excuse for us not to go. Naturally, I didn't tell him about the three dollars I was hoarding.

"You better be back by suppertime," he yelled after us.

When we got to the fairgrounds, the whole town was there: folks with their kids, even babes in arms. We'd saved our appetites for the hot dogs, and we were hungry as bears. The air was full of smells of food, popcorn and cotton candy, and candied apples. We could hardly stand it, our stomachs were growling so. I bought hot dogs for us, all thick with relish and mustard, and we stood there eating them slowly, savoring every bite, each of us trying not to finish before the other. Oh, they were good. And gone too soon.

"You got room for ice cream?" I didn't have to ask. Two scoops of chocolate on sugar cones, nice and cold on the tongue. Great to bite into the top and lick around the sides. We walked around the midway working them down to the last bite of the sugar cone with just a drop of chocolate left in. We had a good time eyeballing the toys and food in the booths, not paying any attention to the other kids who'd come with their grownups.

"This here's a pretty sorry little outfit," an old man behind me was saying to a plump little gray-haired woman in a blue print dress, likely his wife. "Not like the old days. You shoulda seen the geeks that bit off the heads of chickens. Only the ones that did the snakes were even better."

"Yuck—who'd want to do that?"

"The public loved it. When I was a young guy down in Florida, some of us would go out in the swamps and collect snakes for the sideshows. Needed a lot of them, the geeks biting off so many heads—I myself got twenty of them for that season. I knew one guy liked to eat the snakes afterwards. Just fried 'em up. Said it was better than eating chicken."

She stopped and looked him in the face. "Roscoe, you're turning my stomach."

The Kid stared at her belly to see how it was behaving but couldn't see what was happening down there. The old man just grinned at her and went on talking about the great fat ladies he'd seen and the Alligator Man with his scaly skin and some tall guy so thin he didn't look like he had any insides. All kinds of strange things. Some of it sounded pretty creepy.

The woman kept saying, "Oh, stop it, Roscoe."

And he kept saying, "Aw, come on—It's good for the freaks. Gives them regular employment. Lets them become solid citizens. And taxpayers. Better than having them sitting around on their backsides, sponging off other folks."

We'd done a good job on the hot dogs and ice cream, so now for the show. I laid up a big bag of popcorn to hold us up during the performance and went inside and found seats in the front row.

Rags was already out there, working up the crowd, challenging people in the audience to throw pieces of popcorn at him to see if he could catch them in his mouth. He was leaping and catching them and taking bows, getting people ready to laugh. I threw a piece of popcorn in his direction, and he caught it sure enough. The Kid let out a yell and threw one, too, then another. For a little kid, he had a throwing arm you wouldn't believe. And Rags caught those, too.

You could tell the Kid was bowled over—all the lights and smells and people as excited as we were. When they started with the chivaree, I thought he might jump out of his skin the way he bounced up and down. When he saw the elephant lumber in with the red-headed Melba on her back, all in her plumes and pearly costume, he was wild with joy. He waved at her and she blew him a kiss.

63

"It's so big," he cried. "Is that her nose hanging down?" A kind of high-stepping music brought them in. Jessie was there with her python, riding in a chariot pulled by a large bay horse. I just wanted to cry, it was so grand.

Magic—and more magic—the whole show. Came the acrobats who made their pyramids, standing on each others' shoulders till you marveled at all the weight they were holding up; Jessie, taking time with her snake as it moved over her body—the audience hardly able to take it in; the jugglers sending pins and hoops into the air till your eye couldn't follow; and the horses dancing in, their riders in black shirts with silver buttons and pants with silver spangles down the sides, standing on their horses' backs as they raced around the ring, slipping down under the horses' bellies and coming up the other side, while the animals raced at top speed. You just held your breath, it was so scary.

I had my heart in my throat all during the high wire act, even though the man rode his cycle like it was the easiest thing to do, even with a young girl standing on his shoulders. And she didn't seem to mind at all. No nets to catch them if they fell.

Then the trapeze act. There was the lovely woman in blue tights, sequins all over just like in the poster, holding onto the man's wrists, as he was hanging by his knees from the swing. And once she did a backward summersault in mid-air and the man caught her—ZIP, just like that. The whole audience let out a gasp like they'd been punched in the gut—she'd so taken them by surprise. I'd have given anything to be able to do that.

Rags was in and out, putting parts together of strange gadjets that just fell apart, trying to play a trumpet with another clown on a violin, and getting tricked by one of the dogs. He kept the audience in stiches.

Then it was over, and I felt all hollow inside—I just wanted it to never end. It was worse than a movie being over, having to get up from the bleachers we were sitting on, even though our bottoms ached, and make ourselves go out into the daylight with everybody else.

All gone—the lights, the costumes, and performers doing things you couldn't believe. I'd never seen the Kid looking so dreamy and far away. We didn't say a word to one another, just tried to hold onto all that glory for another minute.

The next morning when I got up, I tried to seize hold of what we'd seen. Tried to relive it all, but there were the chickens and the snake, Priam and the Kid to push into the day. The Kid was so grumpy you couldn't even look at him.

"What's the matter?" I asked him. "You having a bad day?"

"YES." "How come?"

"Because there's no circus in it."

Seemed like things would never be the same.

VII.

No, things weren't the same. It was like a stroke of lightning had gone through the atmosphere separating before and after. The circus had made all the difference. It was a shooting star streaking through space, sending off sparks in all directions. Something you'd never seen before that takes you beyond all the sky you know.

Things you had no notion belonged in the same pot began mixing together in ways you never expected. At first you couldn't say any one thing was back of it—that it only had to do with that piece of land Priam had got by hook or crook. The place where the ill-fated roadside zoo had had its brief career. Or that it had all come from Priam's notebook.

You couldn't figure for a long time that it had anything to do with the sheriff. Big old tall drink of water—face pitted and scarred up from acne. Billings. D. W. Nobody ever said his real name, if he had one. Maybe his mama couldn't figure out what it was she'd brought into the world and what to do when it got there. Just there he was, in my life, too—sheriff—dropping in on it, you could never say when. He'd just swing by like he'd accidentally found himself in the neighborhood, park his big sheriff's car, amble over and say, "Howdy, little lady. How's it all going today?" and reach out for my hand with his big meaty paw. "Your granddaddy hereabouts?" His hand would have made two or three of mine.

It was only after you remembered almost stumbling over Priam, that day at the fairgrounds, that you could say any of it was linked to the circus. Meanwhile, the two of them, Priam and D.W., sitting there at the kitchen table, acted like they'd known one another since they popped out of the womb. They made the liquor store a little richer because Priam kept a bottle of hooch on hand for whenever the sheriff stopped by.

"Take a seat, D.W., and have a drop," he'd say, pointing out a chair where the seat wasn't cracked or the legs coming loose, looking like it might collapse any time. "Good for what ails you." They'd sit there and yak and hee-haw and add up figures and do little drawings.

"And once the insurance pays up, I'll get hold of Martinez. That dude owes me a favor," the sheriff he says.

"Good work, D.W.," Priam he says. And they'd pour out another round.

"I figure the labor'll come pretty cheap, if you know what I mean."

One night out of the clear blue, the pens across the road broke into flames, the tall dry grass catching into a blaze, sparks popping everywhere. Then the shed in back of the shack shot up with a roar and phoom! there goes the shack itself.

"Better than a fireworks display," Priam says. I was scared it was going to blow across the road and set us on fire, too. Even though the fire truck was there lickety split, the wood was so dry it was hardly wood anymore, and there wasn't much left except blackened posts and charred ends, with a strong burn smell filling the air.

Next day some fellow drove out to inspect the damage. Then maybe a week later, a couple of Mexicans cleared off the charred ends and whatever else needed hauling away. Pretty soon there was a cement mixer and trucks with cement brick and two-by-fours and big sheets of plywood and lots of other building stuff. Men pouring a foundation, putting up studs, then a frame. Walls going up. I kept watching the changes, sneaking over now and then when nobody was around, to see what was going on. I walked through the foundation, looking at where they'd divided the space into rooms. I watched as they put in a stairway and built the upstairs, set out the roof frame and laid on the tiles, put in the doors and locked them. I listened to the men hammering and sawing and running their drills. They were used to the Kid and me hanging around when I got the chance. A few things were starting to fit together, though I still didn't have any real idea what it all meant. My curiosity was all livened up, that was for sure.

"Somebody going to live there?" I asked Priam, hoping it could be us. Then I could have a room of my own.

"Smart gal," he said. "You got that one nailed down."

"Who?"

"That's for me to know and you to find out. Curiosity killed the cat."

Could've traveled to Timbuktu and back before I did find out. I watched trucks come out with boxes of tile and rolls of carpet, shelves, and bar stools, boxes of lights. One from Freddie's Auction Barn with a big refrigerator and stove. The next time I wandered over, I asked if I could see the inside, and a fellow they called Manny let me in. The downstairs was filled with tables and chairs, one side with a counter lined with bar stools, a big mirror behind the countertop. But what set me to wondering was the little stage on the other side.

The only bar I knew about was the Longhorn Bar in town, where you could look into a dark narrow cave, with men hunched over their whiskeys and beers along the line of bar stools. The reek of beer mixed with dead cigarette butts hit you every time you walked past, hanging over the sidewalk like it was part of the weather. A rough place, especially on Saturday nights—lots of fights, sometimes a knifing that sent somebody to the hospital holding his guts inside, though the bar was right next to the police station.

Priam was all business now, over at the new place or buzzing around town like a horsefly over fresh meat. I didn't know there was that much energy in him, he was usually so occupied with laying around just waiting for things fall into his lap. Now we hardly saw him, which was fine with me and the Kid. We could do what we pleased, so long as the chickens were fed and the snake taken care of.

Meanwhile, all the things that looked like they had nothing to do with one another were snapping together like magnets.

Late one afternoon when it was coming on suppertime, I rode into town because we were out of macaroni and I wanted to stop at the bakery, too. I always got their day-old and sometimes if they had a pastry or two left over, they'd give them to me. If it was only one, I'd save half for the Kid and eat the rest on the way home. That day they had two. When I got outside, a man, kind of scruffy-looking, who'd been leaning near the window said, "Hello, Cutie. Don't think I've seen you here before."

I didn't like the way he was looking at me so I pretended I didn't hear. Just put the bread in the basket and started to get on my bike, when he grabbed hold of the handlebars.

"Hey looka here—Miss Prissy," he said. "I talk to you real nice and you treat me like spit on the sidewalk."

"I got to get home," I said. "Let me go, please." I tried to yank away the handlebars; but he yanked back.

"I'll tell you what. You do me a little favor . . ."

"Let her go, Mister." Came a deep throaty voice. "You hear me? Otherwise I got friends that can hurt you real bad."

I hardly kept the bike from falling as he shoved it away.

"Don't get me wrong, lady. I didn't mean no harm."

"Then clear out." And she swept him off like a cockroach that had crawled too close. She was taller than he was and looked like she could knock him over with one blow. I was really seeing her for the first time, big and handsome, with a thick rope of black hair swept up around her head. Wide cheekbones that made shadows beneath and dark eyes full of fire. She told me later she was part Cherokee. I thought she was the most beautiful woman I'd ever seen. It was Jessie from the circus.

He threw her a finger and slunk off down the street, while I stood there gaping. "You're still here," I stammered.

"No, I been away and now I'm back."

"Where's the circus?"

She shrugged. "Off in the wild blue yonder, for all I care. Work you to death, then starve you for your pains. I got better places for my talents. Well, honey, you better get moving before it gets dark and another one of those low-lifes shows up." She gave me a wink and a wave. "Be seeing you," she said, "with snakes on. That's me at my best."

I watched her as she crossed the intersection with the flagpole in the center and the bank and drugstore, the little Mexican restaurant, and the stationery shop on the corner, and disappeared past the hotel. She moved forward like whatever was in her path had better get out of her way, like she was parting the waters. A chill went down my spine. I hadn't seen anybody like that before.

I wanted to be just like her, moving forward with a swing to the hips in a beautiful set of curves, the way a serpent moves—like she knew exactly where she headed, no stopping her.

It was already twilight when I got back. The Kid was waiting for me, sucking on a spoonful of peanut butter. I put together the macaroni with lots of cheese, and we finished things off with the pastries afterwards. Priam didn't show up that night, and we laid on the couch, teasing and tickling and laughing till we wore ourselves out. We didn't see Priam till late the next afternoon.

He was full of beans, so pleased with himself it's a wonder he didn't bust a suspender.

"We'll bring back the old West in its heyday," he boasted. "Bar, entertainment, and ladies, real lookers, to give you welcome. Just the way things ought to be."

There were neon lights across the entryway now. *The Kitty Kat*, with a big black cat walking away and waving her tail. Girls, girls, girls—flashing on and off.

And sure enough, Jessie was there with her snakes on—one of them a dozen feet long and thicker than my arm. The other two were six feet, much easier to manage. Melba was on hand, too, now part of the act, doing a bit of pantomime, making like she was so scared of the snakes she could hardly stand it. She got the audience to laughing fit to kill. She came on while Jessie was changing her costumes, and she handled the props and helped take care of the snakes. Then she and Jessie teamed up for an act together. She was different from Jessie, but I liked her too. I loved her wild red hair and green eyes that shot right into you when she was fired up, telling you whatever was on her mind, hands going in all directions.

"Glad to be here. Got rid of that woman-chasing s.o.b. husband of mine. Drank, too. I prefer the snakes, let me tell you." She had a laugh that could fill a room and made you want to laugh, too.

Other girls were in the show as well, who didn't feature snakes, but did belly dancing and stripping and were there to hang around the bar to honey up the men when they weren't doing their stuff.

The neighborhood was pretty hopping after the grand opening, cars filling the parking lot, music blaring away, cars stopping and going till all hours.

It turned out I got to see more of the inside of The Kitty Kat than I ever expected. Priam had figured a way to get some work out of me helping Georgia in the kitchen or with the housecleaning. The Kid never wanted to go over there, so he spent a lot more time by himself, I did whatever needed doing at the club—scrubbing floors and counters and cleaning toilets that sometimes smelled of puke and nearly turned your stomach.

My favorite thing was to help Alabama with the cooking. She was the first colored woman I'd ever seen—maybe the only one in town. Her skin was darker than the Mexicans' and she was taller. I liked the way her teeth shone out so white against her dark skin when she laughed. She had an easy laugh and wiggled her shoulders when something struck her funny. And her eyes would light up. But she wouldn't take any guff from anybody, not even Priam, and she told him where to get off at when he tried to skimp on the groceries.

I loved being in the kitchen with her. She made the best fried chicken and pork chops I ever ate, and her chocolate and her lemon meringue pies were a miracle. She taught me about baking and the virtues of lard for piecrust. I'd try to watch how she fluted the crust of a pie and the way she cooked meats and made vegetables tasty, so I could do such things. All the while, she was telling me all about her grown daughters, Carrie and Letty, and their families in Kentucky—and about her uncle who'd become a cowboy in West Texas and another one way back who'd fought with the Buffalo Soldiers in the Civil War. She said her great-grandmother was a slave and had some of her children sold away from her that she never saw again.

Sometimes the girls came to her for advice and comfort. "Whatsa matter, baby?" she'd say. "Tell me why you looking so blue."

Once I asked her, "Was your father named George or did you come from Georgia?"

She just laughed and said, "Maybe one or the other, or both." She liked to tease me. Actually, she came from Alabama, I found out, so I started calling her Alabama. And then Bama. Somehow it suited her.

When I finished my chores, I'd visit Jessie and the other girls late in the afternoon, when they were getting themselves together, sitting around drinking coffee and smoking up a storm, painting their fingernails or toenails and doing up their hair, getting ready for a long night while they hashed over the night before. Mostly they talked about men in a way that made me think I didn't want any part of them.

"I think Pinos Altos has got a crush on you, Melba. Or is it Penis Altos?" They laughed.

"If he does, he sure isn't putting out. One drink and that's it. Tighter than a tick. I'm not holding my breath till he buys me a diamond."

I'd seen what the women in the Westerns were like, hanging around the men in the saloons, but I didn't really catch on to what was going on at The Kitty Kat—for a while. I thought it was all entertainment, with some of the women hunting husbands. But even after I learned they were selling their favors to the men, what really hit me in the slats was most of them were no better off than I was. They'd landed there because they couldn't find a better way to survive. Up the hard way—no father in the house or one that beat on the kids, a mother who was sick or crazy or drunk all the time and couldn't cope. Poor as dirt—and nothing for a future. A couple of them had run away from home by the time they were my age, fourteen or fifteen. One had been on the streets since she was twelve.

Louise said she just counted her lucky stars to be where she was, glad to have a roof over her head and food in her belly—not have to be on the street, bullied by some pimp. Nellie, though, couldn't hide her homesickness. She had a little boy, Bobby, she'd left with her grandmother in Kansas who sent Nellie photos now and then, and Nellie'd show them around, collecting raves—

"Oh, he's adorable. Looks just like you."

"What a sweetheart—that smile."

It gave her a lift for a moment. She had a picture of him in a frame on her dresser, and she'd sit there studying it. Sunday afternoons she talked to her kid on the phone, asking him all about what he'd been doing and whether he liked the cars she'd sent him and telling him how much she loved him.

Jessie was in charge. Except for Yvonne and Sallie who were part of the entertainment with Melba, and Nellie, and Louise who was older, the rest of the women came for maybe six months and then moved on somewhere else. The men liked variety, Jessie said, and it was good to have new faces, "as though that made any difference," she said. She ran the place with a steady hand. She'd had some money saved up and put it into the business. She had a good head for the money side and didn't allow for any nonsense. She was good to her little pusses, as she sometimes called them. She didn't baby them and she wouldn't stand for drinking or dope. Their drinks were sodas or tea, and they made a big profit on them. Pretty high prices for the regular drinks, too. That came with the entertainment.

Jessie treated me like I was one of the family, and when she found out Priam wasn't paying me hardly anything for my work ("I'm saving it for you till you're eighteen and get your walking papers"), she went to bat for me. She went with me to open a savings account and she helped me keep track of things.

I liked the other women, except for the newcomers, Ledalia and Renata, who thought they were the Kitty Kat's meow because of their good looks and because they brought in more men than the others. They looked at Louise like she was a charity case. But they all looked up to Jessie, because she was fair-minded and wouldn't squeeze her girls for the last nickel. She gave them advances, too, out of her own pocket if they got into trouble and were desperate for cash. Louise, who must have been in her forties—she seemed old to me—was supporting her mother in Tennessee, who had bad heart trouble, was in and out of the hospital. Jessie helped her out.

Although Jessie agreed with Melba that she liked her snakes better than any of the men that came around, she had her admirers. "I was married once—long enough for me to know I'd never want to do that again," she told me. But she acted like she enjoyed the company of the guys who bought her drinks, and she'd sit at their tables if she wasn't onstage. There was one fellow, older than her, in his fifties, with silver in his sideburns and a silvery mustache, who came around just for her company. He was an important man in the state legislature, one of the girls said, and he gave her anything she wanted. That's how come she drove a bright white Cadillac.

Wow! I thought. Seemed like a good sort of man to have.

He'd take her to the one fancy club in town, where you could get a good steak and dance to a band on weekends. It caused a stir, but he didn't give a hoot who saw him, and Jessie liked to laugh about it. When you saw her all dolled up, she came on like she was a celebrity. Stopped you dead in your tracks.

Sometimes I watched her take off her makeup and when she'd got it all off, she looked different, still beautiful, but not like she'd been. She knew how to do things to herself that made her so stunning you couldn't take your eyes off her.

But it was part of the picture—her smile, her laugh, the way she moved. All together, she was a show-stopper.

For her act she put on false eye lashes and wove sequins into her hair. She made up her own outfits, some lacy and see-through that seemed to reveal everything, but even though they teased you into looking at her breasts or her crotch, kept something hidden that would never be revealed. Other costumes of red and blue fit tight around her waist and made almost overflowing cups of her breasts.

"That's where it all begins," she said to me with a laugh. "Welcome to the world."

For her act, she slipped off one layer of her costume a piece at a time, letting the colors and textures play off one another until she was all there in the next layer, the audience clapping, eager for more. It was a show in itself—until she was down to the last little teasers that barely covered her nipples, her sex. She'd stand there in her platform heels, letting everybody admire her, gathering their eyeballs, as she put it. Then she'd move over to the innocent-looking wicker basket at the side of the stage and let out her python.

From the audience, a gasp. They'd forget about her for a moment, as they took in what they were seeing, just its being there—SNAKE— and a big one or maybe two, OH MY GOD!—From that point on, it was all about her and the snake, and what was she going to do with it? Then they'd go into the dance together.

I could see she was in a different place, the look on her face as though nobody else was there and only one thing filled the space, herself and the snake, the place where they flowed together. And that place was power. I knew I had to get there too.

It didn't matter what she was doing, my eyes were on her, taking in every move and waiting for the next. She was more than one person. You'd see her with the girls, you'd see her with the men, and then you watched her with the snakes.

She had it all together, but for me it was one big juggling act. Trying to keep an eye on the Kid and see he got fed, him and Priam, and the chickens and the python. I got to where I'd take the Kid over to the house with me, and Nellie would pay attention to him, because he reminded her of her son. She'd do puzzles and play checkers and crazy eights with him. I'd bring him books and I bought him Lincoln logs and paints to keep him busy. He still spent time down at the arroyo.

I was so busy it seemed like I could hardly keep hold of whatever was me. It all went bumping along till one day, I got caught up short.

That morning when I went to pee, I looked down and saw brown stuff like I'd never seen before in my panties, and I didn't know what it was. If it was blood . . . did it mean I was sick and going to die? I walked around scared. What was wrong with me? I didn't know what to do, or who to ask about it. At first, I thought I'd ask Bama, but she was banging pots and pans around in the kitchen because Priam had put her in a mood, pretty fierce it looked like—high up it was on the scale of bad moods. Sometimes just looking at him was enough to give you the blues for the rest of the week.

Finally, I worked up the nerve to ask Jessie. She just laughed and gave me a hug. "Why, Lovey, you're a woman now. Great day. Hey, Louise, Nellie." She called them over. "We've got a new woman here." I must have turned pink and purple, as they laughed and hugged me and told me, "Welcome to the club. You've got your moons—how about that."

"This little chick needs some educating," Jessie said, "—what you'd get if you had a mama." She took me to town and wised me up along the way. "Birds do it, bees do it," she sang, "even educated fleas do it. And you need a little equipment." She took me to the drugstore for Tampax to keep on hand, and then to Penny's to shop around. "It's about time you had a bra," she said, "just to get used to the idea."

I tried on a few till I found one that was comfortable. When I looked in the mirror, I felt strange.

"Don't worry," she said, "you got a bit of developing to do. This is just a start." I realized that part of my watching her was trying to figure out what it was like to be a woman. It was all very confusing.

"I want to be just like you," I told her, thinking I'd never make it. "Only you're beautiful."

"You just need a few tricks. Nature isn't about to give you everything for nothing," she said. "Oh, maybe a few touches—but there's nothing says you can't go off on your own—improvise. Make yourself into something special that calls out loud and clear. Even people who have no looks to speak of can be stunning."

I'd tried putting on a little lipstick, once in a while, but my hair was dishwater color, and the mirror told me I was nothing out of the ordinary.

"You come over tomorrow afternoon, and I'll show you a thing or two," she said. "You'll be a different creature."

I went home all in a dream, almost forgot to look both ways crossing the road. I could hardly sleep, thinking about what she might do with me.

The next afternoon she sat me down in front of her mirror so I could watch the whole shebang. "We'll start with the basics, just so you can see." She put a light base on my face, then started brushing in some contours so there were little shadows under my cheek bones, like hers. "You got nice cheekbones—they just need a little accenting." Then she did some green eye shadow under my eyes and put on some dark lashes. She painted my lips a deep rose. Then she made two little scallops of hair down towards my ears and pulled the rest back and rolled it over a rat and curled it up into a chignon. I hardly recognized myself.

"See," she said. "You're gorgeous. Old Priam wouldn't recognize you."

"Oh, don't let him see me," I begged her.

"'Course I wouldn't. The old buzzard would probably have you turning tricks. This is just to show you what you can do—not yet though. Just be a girl for a while."

Every once in a while now, I'd see Priam's eye on me—just like the old witch in Hansel and Gretel, waiting till they were fat enough to pop in the oven.

Most of the time he'd seen me with my hair wild from the wind, streaks of dirt across my cheek, and mud on my clothes. I'd always been a tomboy, but nature had other plans for me. I just kept filling out, getting a waistline. I grew more the year I was fifteen than I had any other year. I was almost as tall as Jessie, though not as big-boned.

When I was sixteen or thereabouts, I looked a couple of years older than I was. After it all came together, I realized Jessie had plans for me she wasn't telling me about. First she hired a Mexican girl to help Bama with the household chores and then started me waitressing at the tables in the evenings two or three nights a week. I was getting tips, and that made it a easier for me to squirrel away a fair amount that Priam didn't get his mits on. After Melba told Jessie she was leaving to marry a cattle dealer from Kansas City who kept coming back to court her, Jessie began prompting me, trying to build up my confidence.

I'd been watching the two of them with their snake-dancing all along, and sometimes I tried a few things on my own with Pajarito. Jessie had me bring him over a time or two and watched me handle him. She started giving me suggestions. Then she started letting me handle her snakes, too, the smaller ones. One day, not long before Melba left, she said to me, "You know snakes like they're your cousins. You can handle them better than anybody I know. What do you say about taking Melba's place?"

The very thought made me tremble. It was like I'd been asked to be queen. But more than that, it was the idea of standing in front of an audience, trying to be like Jessie.

"That's great," she said even before I could deliver an answer. My face must have given me away—of course, I wanted to do it, scary though it was.

"I think you need a little ritual by way of initiation." She showed me a tattoo she had on her upper thigh, not a snake exactly, but a little spiral. I didn't know what to think about it.

The next day we set off for town; she was taking me to Mooney's Tattoo parlor, a little place down Bent Street, more like an alley than a street—no sidewalks and muddy when it rained. Like the place was hiding there. Lots of people didn't favor tattoos and would have been glad to close it down.

"What do you think?" she said, as we looked at the poster in front, an elaborate heart with an arrow going through. "It hurts like fury, but it'll never come off. Your signature. He'll do whatever you want, not just copy something out of a book."

If Jessie could do it, I figured I had to do it, too. Inside was Mooney, a slender, wiry fellow with curly black hair and a black beard, and tattoos all down his arms. The walls of the tattoo parlor were covered with photos of people Mooney had done. Like a picture gallery: men and women showing off their arms and backs, parts of their chests, their legs and torsos. Some of them looked like movie stars. Mooney said he'd been in L.A. for a while and had done just about everything in the way of tattoos—even a wolf coming out of some guy's ass. Body painting and girlie tattoos and whole galaxies. He unbuttoned his shirt to show us animals and birds and plants twining in and out, then on his back, sun, moon, and planets. Seemed like he was carrying the whole universe on his body.

He wore a bracelet and an earring to set things off. They looked good on him. He had friends in the business, he told us, and he had studied under two artists he spoke of like they were stars.

"Some of the best in the country," he said. "They taught me everything I know. They did all my tattoos," he said.

"What would you like?" he asked me. "What you put on your body gives a hint of what you are or what's really important to you."

I just looked at him, kind of blank—it was a big idea.

"It's serious business," he said, with a smile. "There are some books you can look through," he said, pointing to a shelf—"or just let something come to you."

At first I thought of a tiger, because of Antoinette. Then Pajarito. They went deep, all right—part of me. But they belonged to me in a different way. I knew I wanted something with wings. "A butterfly," I said. "Could you do one—right here on my belly?"

"Pretty sensitive spot. How about something small?" he suggested.

"It doesn't have to be big." I just liked thinking of having it there. "What color?"

"Blue," I said. I didn't know if there were blue butterflies.

"Down in Peru," he said. "They got big blue ones, but they have little ones too. It'll show up nice."

It did hurt like fury, and I was glad when he was finally done.

"Congratulations," Jessie said. "'You passed the test." So I went home with my butterfly. I kept looking at it in the mirror. I felt different. That evening, Jessie gave me a little wine for the occasion.

"You're on your way, girlfriend, " she said, the next afternoon when she was getting things together for her performance. "Snakes will be your meal ticket, believe me."

She was studying me. "Now we got to give you a real stage name," she said. She'd always called me Lovey or Darling. I'd told her my name was secret, and she didn't make a big deal over it.

But now I figured it was time to tell her. "I have my special name," I said, the name I sometimes wrote over and over, like it was some sort of charm. "It's Grace," I waited to see how it grabbed her.

She took it in with an expression like she'd seen a gleam in a gold pan. "Grace," she said, lingering over the syllable. "Amazing Grace—absolutely perfect."

"No," I said. "Nothing amazing about it. It's just my name." I hadn't thought what would happen going public with it.

"Go on. If you haven't got there yet, you'll get there one way or the other—count on it. You're plugging into your future, Babe. Just let the juices flow."

It was scary.

"Listen to me, kid," she said. "You gotta take all the help you can get. It's tough out there. You know what I'm doing?—I'm saving my money. Just socking it away, and when I get enough, I'm heading to California, maybe stop a while at Vegas on the way."

We were in her room. She was sitting in front of the mirror, brushing her hair. It came all the way down to her waist, so black it looked blue, full of lights. I envied her that hair.

"I want to land on the near side of paradise, where I can have the kind of life I've always dreamed of. Maybe find a good man—if there's one still out there—and have a piece of property in a beautiful spot—horses and maybe a mountain to look at and some water flowing."

I could imagine her getting what she wanted. Would that happen for me? I hardly dared think about it.

"You don't want to turn tricks, do you?"

"I'd hate it." Most of the men I saw put me off, even though some didn't look like bad sorts. Some of them were big shots in town—like the sheriff, who spent a lot of time there. But the way the women talked, the men looked down on them, like scrapings from the pot. Treated them like they were throwaways.

"That's where I started, but I got out of that soon as I could—Give me the managing end every time."

"Come here a minute." She did a few more touches with my hair, trying to style it a new way and stood back to get the full effect.

"I will say there's money in it, kid, if you got the right connections. Vegas to one of those fancy places, you can make yourself a pot, but you got to go for the rich types."

"I want to go to school," I said. "I want to go to high school, maybe even college." I didn't know what I expected, but I wanted it, whatever it was, in the worst way. And I knew I couldn't do anything till I was eighteen and had some money. I had trouble holding onto whatever I got, because the Kid and I both needed things. Otherwise we'd have been in rags. I never knew what Priam did with his money except drink it up.

She gave me a long look. "Well, one way or another you're going to have to earn your way. That old buzzard'll pick you clean and leave your carcass to the crows. So watch out."

She didn't have to warn me. Whatever dream was going through my head, Jessie always put me back right there on solid ground. You start out dreaming—it just comes with the territory—and it's hard work keeping hold of what's in front of your eyes. The dreaming gets in your way. Jessie was on target. Leaving home had never left my mind. But where would I go and what could I do on the streets? Besides, there was the Kid—I couldn't just leave him to go wild. If I went, he'd have to go too. And I wanted to get there dancing.

I'd worn Pajarito around my shoulders a lot, walked around with him, let him coil around my arms, my waist, my thighs, but though I kept trying to imitate Jessie, I had no real idea about dancing with a snake. That is, it seemed to me there was a kind of X quality you had to have before it was any good.

"You're halfway there," Jessie told me, "because you're not scared and that snake trusts you. You just got to go slow with them, let them show you the way."

Although she'd been teaching me things from the beginning, now she concentrated on how you can work up interest using a veil, taking a basket with the snake inside and drawing away the veil and letting the snake slowly emerge from the basket and crawl across the floor. I spent a lot of time practicing, bending over and letting Pajarito crawl up my arm, taking him in my hands and doing a backbend holding up the snake. Letting him twine around my shoulder and down my arm to my waist. After that, I practiced with Jessie. Though Pajarito was only about five feet long, he was a lot of snake to handle. Jessie had one big albino snake she'd dance with by itself, but she had two that were around six feet, so I'd work with them too.

Jessie had me start things off. Then she would take over, the featured part of the act, and following her, the strippers. Then she and I would come on together for the finale. After the show, Jessie would weave around among the tables and along the bar, joking with the men, putting her arm around their shoulders. They loved it. "Now I want you to keep an eye out for my little protégée," she'd say. "If you

81

don't come forward with a little do-re-mi, I'll drop a snake on your table." Then she'd laugh.

The guys and sometimes the women would laugh, too. I don't know if she'd actually have done it—she had high respect for her snakes—but she made her point. After the act was over and my snake back in the basket I'd walk around the tables myself.

"You got to flirt with them a little," she told me. "That's what they're paying for. Don't hang back. Entertainment value. There's a power in you, and you've got to learn how to use it. That's all there is to it. Use it or it'll turn on you—come back and bite you in the butt."

So I tried it out. The take was pretty good.

Both Priam and the sheriff were around a lot "checking on things, making sure the operation ran smooth," and they didn't miss a trick.

"I never thought that snake was worth a piss in the pot," Priam said. "In fact, I thought you put one over on me. But he's worth money, that's for sure."

I may have saved his beautifully patterned hide, but I still wasn't sure about my own.

VIII.

I loved the dancing. You have to keep your mind on the snakes—you've got to learn their temperaments. The Burmese are pretty mellow, especially the lighter colored ones. You don't want to startle them, though. You have to let them go where they're tending and follow along, slowly, and know when to guide them. So my dance was a little different every time, a different creation, a pattern we made together with the music. Nobody was there but the snakes and me and what we were creating together. There was a hush when the snakes emerged from the basket and when I linked them over my arms and they coiled around them. Eyes held us, but we weren't there. It was like dreaming.

The Kitty Kat was a popular place. They came from all around—from Copperville and Santa Anna and Kingston. Sometimes from up north when visitors came down this way. Cowboys and miners and town folks. And some important people from around the state, who knew Jessie and thought highly of her. At first some of the guys acted like snake-dancing was pretty weird and off-the-wall. They were used to killing any snake they saw. Besides, they'd mostly come to get a few beers, and some sweet meat. But there was a kind of fascination—a woman taking up an honest-to-god snake and dancing with it.

And Jessie was the big draw, as beautiful to watch in action as to look at. She'd started out as a belly dancer, and then took on the snakes and did her circus act. A real performer. A new little snake she'd bought she wore around her head like a crown, another around her shoulders, hips slowly undulating. She could send chills up and down your spine. Sometimes she just held out her arms, a snake in each hand, just stood there with the stillness. And a hush would rise in the audience. She held them in her spell whether she was still or moving, the snakes and her body one flowing movement. Maybe it got all their juices flowing out there, men and women alike, something deep down that made them want to enter in, let their own bodies find a few moves of their own.

I wanted her to show me the ropes, tell me what to do so I could get it right. She was willing. But it was more than that. I could tell she was somewhere way beyond me. She had a knowing. She'd got to places I hadn't reached. And I wanted to. Envy would never get you there, I knew that too. I could only learn from her what she could teach. Then I'd have to find my way on my own. I couldn't just be her creation.

The "hostesses" were good at what they did, too. And it was more than just cadging drinks, trying to get a buck. Jessie had her ideas about that. "Listen to them," she told the girls. "Let them talk. You'll be hearing things they don't tell their wives."

For a dusty little hole of a mining town, The Kitty Kat was big entertainment. Once every two weeks they had a dance out at the club, as they called it. Lots of couples came and you'd see the cars lined up along the road for half a mile in both directions. There were a half a dozen bars in town where you could get drunk or pick a fight or both, and feed quarters into the juke box. There were dances out at a big barn that drew a crowd. But the Kitty Kat had everything.

Seems like I practically lived over there. You could say I got my education from being there. I heard a lot of woman talk, no holds barred—about their experiences with men, about their growing up, their lives, their alcoholic parents, their poverty and hard times, the troubles with their kin. They'd sit and tell their stories by the hour. I'd seen enough of Priam's girlie mags and heard enough talk to smarten me up about what went on that most people didn't want to talk about. Some of it was pretty terrible.

One day, Jessie said to me, "Tell me, Lovey, have you ever got your feet wet?" I knew what she was talking about. I shook my head.

"I figured. That's why you've got that edge of shyness around men—you've not had any experience. We've got to do something about that."

"I do better with snakes."

She laughed. "I get your message," she said. "But don't close the door too soon. There are men who know how to treat a woman. I know a young man I think you'd like, and he's a good lover."

"How do you know?" She'd startled me and made me curious as all get-out.

"I taught him," she said. "Once upon a time, his dad was sweet on me—we had our innings. Now we're just friends. A while back, he wanted me to smarten up his son a little. College student. A good kid. Manly, but not a stud."

"You mean I'd do it for money?"

"No," she said, "not unless you have a craving for cash. Hell, I was fourteen when a guy popped my cherry. Twenty years older than me. That's what comes of being around a bunch of sexed up males." She gave me a sharp look, like she'd pulled a few memories from the files. "You think that's what you want before you know what you're stepping into." She sat tapping her fingers like she was playing a worn-out tune. "But he took care of me, I'll say that for him. And I was on my own. Water under the bridge . . . Anyway this young fellow I'm speaking of is a natural lover. That doesn't happen all that often, and unless you want to hold onto to your virginity until your pubic hair falls out or you get taken by surprise . . . Oh, I know, the old bit of holding yourself pure for marriage. But I'm all for having a little experience under your belt so you know what you're in for—whether you're getting a good lover or not. Somebody who's interested in your pleasure same as his."

She could see I was thinking it over. And my body was sending me a few signals I couldn't ignore but didn't know what to do about.

"I could set you up with a date, and you can decide what'll come of it."

I was both eager and shy. I had a real terror of men. Except for Ralph, way back when. But I was just a kid then. And now I was seventeen. It was exciting, too, to think of meeting somebody near my own age who was going to college. Somebody smart. Only I was afraid he'd see how ignorant I was and look down on me. Afraid of my lack of experience in just about everything.

"Don't be scared," she said. "He'll be just as nervous as you are.

And you got more going for you than you realize. Trust me and I'll set things up the right way."

I did trust her—she was the only one I did trust that deeply. So Jessie had him come out to the Kitty Kat to see me dance. She brought him up to me afterwards behind the scenes and we stood for a moment exchanging chemistries, you might say, and said our hello's. His name was Ben. He was good-looking all right, tall and slender, well-built, with a kind of amusement in his expression. He made me smile; we both smiled. I was trying to look good in a skirt with a gold-and-white pattern and a light green blouse Jessie had helped me shop for, and my hair was coiled up around my head. She had done my makeup with a light touch—"just enough to accent the positive," she said. She'd done the little shadows under the cheekbones.

"That was really terrific," he said after Jessie left us and we were walking towards his car. He'd been sitting up pretty close to the stage, watching the show, but I didn't know who he was or where he was sitting. It was a good thing. I couldn't let my thoughts stray—I had to turn my eyes inside and concentrate on what I was doing. No room for getting nervous then. But I sure was nervous now. Jessie sent us off to the late show in town. But we decided just to go and have a hamburger instead.

He was fascinated seeing me dancing with snakes.

"That sends chills up my spine," he said. "I can't imagine me doing anything like that. It would just send me into the shivers." He did an imitation of what it would do to him and had me laughing. He wanted to know what it was like up there with the snakes coiled around me, and I tried to tell him how it felt, what you had to keep in mind. I tried not to feel stupid. It was good to have someone to tell about it. I liked the way he listened—like he really was interested and really wanted to know me.

It was the first time I'd really talked to a fellow near my age, or felt any attraction for a male, or allowed myself to. He had a good face—a little scar near his chin made it interesting. He had a light in his eyes, and I liked his hands, strong-looking with long fingers.

He took my elbow and led me to the car because it was dark and there were broken spots in the parking lot. It was a new feeling, having someone touch me like that. It made me a little shivery. Especially when he smiled at me. I didn't know how to smile back without its looking phony. I was trying to be easy-going. I liked the idea, but it's hard to make yourself let go and just relax.

The talk went on while we had our hamburgers at the Dairy Queen. I didn't know how to talk about my upbringing, so I let him talk about his. He told me his mother had died when he was seven, and the way the housekeeper his father hired used to punish him by not feeding him. That made it easier to say a few things about myself.

He didn't try to make out when we went back but gave me a kiss that didn't linger and asked if I'd like to go the movies that weekend. Before that, he came out to watch me dance and afterwards Jessie sat and talked with us for a while, asked Ben how his summer was going. He had a job exercising horses at a riding stables. "Better than constuction," he said. "And I get to do some riding."

Then we took off for town for an ice cream before the show started. I had a question for him.

"What's it like to go to college?" It sounded like a stupid question, but I couldn't think of any other way to put it.

"It's good. Lots of new stuff in your life besides what's going on in the classroom."

He described the campus, the design of the buildings had been copied from architecture somewhere in Asia I'd never heard of. Told me how beautiful the library and other buildings were. As he described his classes and teachers, the books he read, it sounded like a whole different world. He told me about his friend Tom, who wanted to study engineering and who played guitar like a pro and made up his own songs; and his roommate, Jordan, who was studying Latin American history and wanted to go to Peru. And Belvin, who drove fancy cars his father bought him—he had money to burn. He liked to speed everywhere, was proud of his speeding tickets, and wrecked a couple of his cars. Ben did an imitation of Belvin asking his father for another new one and had me laughing.

I couldn't imagine such things. "What about you? What do you want to do?"

He looked at me. "Don't know yet. My dad wants me to study law, go into politics." He shrugged. "I don't think I'm made for that. I'd like to do something for kids maybe. I love making up games for them and getting them to tell stories. I like to do puppets. I do a frog with big ideas—wants the find a big pond and run things. Gets into arguments with the ducks." He went into his frog voice and gave me a sample. He had me laughing at that, too. He had put his arm around me.

"I really, really want to go to college," I told him, wishing I could just get to high school.

He told me I should apply—maybe I could get a scholarship and take some tests.

Only how can I? I thought. It was like I'd grown up in the fields with coyotes and rabbits. I told him I'd tried to read the books they read in high school and learn some science and a little math. I read some literature books as well. I'd read *Macbeth* and *Romeo and Juliet*. The language was tough-going—I didn't understand a lot of it, but I liked the sound of it. I loved *Huckleberry Finn* and read it over and over. I traveled down that river right with him and cried when he decided to save Jim even if he went to hell. I figured I'd go there with him. I read everything I could get by Mark Twain, and Ivanhoe, and poems by Robert Frost, and *Gulliver's Travels*. How strange it was! I'd gone lots of places in books.

Ben told me I must be pretty smart to read things like that. But I could only think about how much I'd missed and what I didn't know.

That night he kissed me for real as we stood at the back entrance to the Kitty Kat, a kiss we lingered in till the breath went out of us. I waited till his car disappeared, and I went across the highway to where Priam was still up. I'd hoped to sneak into bed without him noticing. But he was there in front of me like a brick wall.

"Where you been?"

"Nowhere special," I told him. I knew he didn't believe me.

"Well, if you come in wearing your panties around your neck, I guess I'll know what's going on."

I wanted to butt him in the gut. The next morning I hid his girlie magazines out in the chicken coop.

"Don't get any notions about falling in love," Jessie warned me. "I see you got the susceptibility. Well, get it gone. His father's got plans for him, and you're not part of the package, believe me. So be careful. I don't want you getting hurt. He's got his way paved, and you've got a path full of rocks and thorn bushes."

I tried to keep her warning in mind, but I hardly knew what was happening to me. My body was like a flame ignited. It wanted to tumble down the path, wanted it bad, and I wanted that and something more I couldn't give a name to. Some of the romance I saw in the movies, even though it was all playacting.

The rest came easier than I thought. Seemed like he knew when to invite me to leap in. That night, we went out to a motel on the edge of town. Jessie had already given me some contraceptives and instructions. "Don't want you getting pregnant," she said. "Just keep your head.

We had a great time undressing each other a piece at a time, fumbling with buttons, kissing and touching along the way. It had me on fire, but I was scared too. It was like the dancing, you just have to let yourself go with it. But then when I started bleeding, I got scared again. Jessie had told me that would happen, but it's different hearing about it and experiencing it.

"Well," Ben said, after things had quieted down, and I was lying in his arms, "You're not a virgin anymore." It seemed like something to get past and be done with.

Jessie just looked at my face the next day and said, "Welcome to the new club."

After that, Jessie let us use Nellie's room upstairs. She'd gone to Wichita for a few days to visit her son. And I got a lot of teasing from the women.

Ben and I saw a lot of each other for the next little while, snatching our lovemaking when we could, staying up till all hours. I wondered how he or I managed to work the next day. We found new ways to please each other and sometimes laughed at the way things went all on their own, playful and easy.

"You're okay with me then?" Ben said, a time or two.

Okay? I'd learned to feel joy with him.

The night before he left to go back to school, I could hardly keep from crying. He took me out to the Bobcat Club, where we had a steak dinner—it was a pretty fancy place. We listened to Eartha Kitt on the jukebox. We danced and held each other close.

"I'm going to miss you," he said, "—a lot. You're the real thing, you know."

Then he was gone—not so far away in miles, but it could have been as far away as the moon. It was like a deep pit opened up inside me. A whole new set of feelings. A big deep lonely one. I told myself I didn't love him—it was never meant to be more than a passing thing, part of my education, but that didn't seem to help much. Jessie saw me mooning around, though I tried to put on some kind of neutral expression, but she caught me out.

"You trying to look like a piece of cardboard?" she said with a little smile. "You look stiff as one." She studied me while I stood there naked on one foot.

"You think you love him," she said. "Well, you're fresh, with pure feelings, and there's the longing. Whatever the flame lit up. But don't trust it. It's a one-time thing—happens that once, and then it's just an oil spot on the road."

For a moment I just wanted to hit her and tell her she didn't know what she was talking about.

"Oh, I know," she said, not letting go of me—I was ready to cry from her cruelty—"you think you've experienced what nobody else has ever experienced before. And I'm not knocking it. You've been lucky. Just don't put your trust in it."

"Have you ever been in love?" I threw back at her.

"Hell, yes," she said, "Though I doubt you'll believe it, hardened case that I am. Got it bad once. I'll tell you about it sometime."

I'd ask her about it now and then, but somehow she always evaded it. "Let me just say that there was a time I took to target practice, and there's a handy little pistol in my nightstand."

I'd tried to keep my activities a secret from Priam—I knew that

90

Jessie and the others would cover for me. But my hours had become highly irregular. A lot of nights I just slept over at the Club. Turned up the next morning to make breakfast. I was feeling pretty guilty too, not giving a whole lot of time to the Kid. He didn't complain, but I could tell he was happy to see Nellie when she got back.

"Where you been keeping yourself?" Priam'd ask me.

"I had a date," I'd tell him. At that point, lying wasn't going to do me any good.

"Oh, so things are moving in that direction," he said. "I hope some of the guys are treating you real good." He didn't interfere right then or make a big deal of it—he was just biding his time.

Anyway he had other things to keep him all hot and bothered. The mayor and a couple of the councilmen were giving him a hard time. Certain folks thereabouts had complained that the Kitty-Kat was giving the town a bad name, and that Jessie was a disgrace to our community—undermining the morals, corrupting youth. It had Priam storming around.

"Morals," he snorted. "This town hasn't got the morals of a she goat in heat, let alone a *Playboy* fold-out."

But Sheriff Billings was having his hands full trying to keep off "the damned hypocrites," as Priam called them. Now, whenever the sheriff came by, Priam had to put him off, but with kid gloves, so he said. Billings kept pushing for more money to pay off the mayor and the councilmen, the police chief and a man in the hauling business, who was big in one of the churches where the voices were loudest.

Priam had experience keeping a tight fist. "I'm in it to the hilt," he'd argue, with a kind of whine he got in his voice when he had to part with any cash. "Just barely taking in enough for the mortgage, the insurance, the girls, the medics and the booze. Jessie doesn't come cheap. Not to mention the advertising. Had to hock half my soul to get into the Yellow Pages. That's investment money. That's capital. What about you? You're supposed to be keeping the way open."

D.W. just shrugged him off. "If you can't stand the heat, get out of the kitchen. Or take things south."

That was all the incentive Priam needed. The tropical wind was in the air, and he'd caught a whiff of the difference. I was still trying to keep an eye on the Kid and the chickens and everything at the house. But there's no telling how long the idea had been percolating in his brain.

He must've figured I knew it was in the cards. And he'd have to have been pretty thick not to notice Ben coming round the place and me leaving with him. Nor did he take me for a dummy, though he treated me like one. If I was putting out, he'd need one girl less besides nearly all of what I took in.

I'd been hoarding my money, putting it in the savings account Jessie helped me open. I was hoping I could clear out before Priam tried to corner me. I had to do something.

The Kid was getting out of hand. Now that he was old enough to be off on his own, he was wandering around town getting into mischief. I caught him stealing magazines and candy bars, and I was afraid he was going to do something worse.

Jessie and I tried to get him into school, figuring he had too much time by himself. We knew he was smart enough to start at least in the third grade. I'd taught him to read and do arithmetic. He read comics and books about dinosaurs and the planets. We took him to the school, and after they gave him some tests, they were willing to put him in the third grade for a trial period. But from the very first, it looked like a poor idea. Since he was older than the other kids and didn't know how to act, they teased him and bullied him. He refused to sit at his desk. He hit one of the boys who was making fun of him, and a bunch of his older buddies jumped him on the playground and bloodied him up. His teacher, Miss Blake, sent him down to the nurse to get cleaned up, and he just took off right after that.

About that time he quit talking again. It was like he'd gone back to being what he was before, and I couldn't get him to trust me again. I was terrified the school would get after him and they'd come and put him in a foster home.

He'd still go down to the arroyo and make things out of clay and paint them. Sometimes he sang songs about them. But he wouldn't talk, and there were times he threw a fit when I tried to get him to take a bath or brush his teeth. I knew we had to get out of there.

One night after the show, Priam said, "Seems to me it's time for your debut."

I just stared at him. "Now don't give me that holier-than-thou expression. I know what's what. You're a sexy little number," he said in a way that made me cringe. "The guys can smell the scent and they're ready to beat down your door—one of them anyway."

"There isn't anybody anymore." I hadn't had a letter from Ben, didn't expect one.

"Well, there will be. You just have to be on hand. Why there are parts of the world where you start out in the trade when you're five years old. And you're a dozen years beyond that."

It made me furious, him thinking I was just another body to be put up for sale, like I was hardly human. What could I expect? I knew I'd never meant much to him, but it hurt deeper than I imagined.

"Glad Jessie got you going," he said, "I've heard a few compliments." Like we were talking about a new dress. "You'll be a real asset, make a real contribution."

"I'm doing that already," I reminded him. I turned my back on him.

"Look here, you've been no end of trouble to me, and now it's payback time."

"I'm already paying my way," I told him. "And you can't make me."

"You'll do what I say as long as you're under my roof."

I threw him a finger and ran out. It was time for me to run. I could dance, and I figured I could earn something of a living—maybe go to Nevada like Jessie said. And she'd been hearing a lot about Ventura City, one of those Seven Cities of Cibola that a couple of the women came from. A fantastic place—that was the story—somewhere between Mexico and the United States, a place that had fallen out of history but was none the worse for it.

And maybe a lot better, because, Priam said, sometimes History stroked a finger or two over things and left a dirty smudge. Two of the newer women, Tina and Margarita, had told Jessie about their wild life there and the piles of money they'd made and blown. And why hadn't they stayed instead of coming to this dismal little spot on the highway?

"They want the young things," they said. "Sometimes they get them twelve and thirteen—right off the streets."

"You'd make a lot of dough," Tina told me.

Jessie had come up with another scheme.

"I think we could take off some of the heat if we put on a little show downtown," Jessie said. "Snakes and strippers, why not? In the old days before TV and football, strip shows were good entertainment. And I know a couple of dudes from the circus who wouldn't mind coming down for a bit of clowning. Comic routines for the belly laugh and some skin for the eyeballs. Good advertising—might improve the cash flow."

I don't know quite how she managed it, but we got set up to do a show in the old Coyote Theater. It had been bought by an outfit that came in out of El Paso—The Time of Your Life Theaters. They had built two places on the other side of town from the Coyote, one for family entertainment and kiddie audiences and the other, right across the street, for the thrill seekers, the horror lovers, the war film types, and the sex seekers. The Coyote was sitting there dull and empty, smelling of stale popcorn, still waiting for enterprise. It had a stage.

Even Priam thought the show was a great idea. Actually, Jessie had a way of working him up with a little silk and sweet talk, then slipping things past when his usual suspicions weren't kicking in. After she'd softened him up, there were moments when he would sink beneath her gaze. I loved to watch him under her spell.

"I figured the old fart would kick in," Jessie said. She knew her power.

We planned it for the Sunday before the 4th of July, when everybody was getting roused up for a little celebrating, booze, and fireworks. The Kitty Kat was doing its thing in town. Two of Jessie's clown buddies came down from Denver and worked up the crowd, actually a good turnout. One of them stood joking with the audience, while two of our girls pranced out in abbreviated cowgirl outfits: Western hats, and skirts just to the tops of their thighs, and little denim jackets

94

decorated with rhinestones. Cute. They tossed off their hats—the clowns grabbed them up and paraded around in them, cracking jokes, and imitating their moves. Then they admired the jackets that were thrown to them, hugged them like there were women inside, then got more excited about the skirts. When they looked up and saw the gals in their g-strings and pasties, they did feints and pratfalls all over the stage, and finally cartwheeled off while the women shimmied and bounced and did their bumps and grinds.

We followed with snakes on, Jessie first with her albino, Alba, and a new one, a boa constrictor she'd ordered from a catalog—just had to have her. A couple of women in the audience got up and made for the exit quick as they could go—not snake types. But everyone else was mesmerized.

Next it was me. This time I had two snakes. Jessie thought it would be a good idea for me to take turns with her pythons for awhile, since she was all involved with her boa. It was a challenge for me all right, on account of being in front of a much larger audience. I felt nervous up there on the stage, but I took a couple of deep breaths and put my attention where it belonged.

I opened the basket and carefully lifted up Pajarito and let him crawl up my arm and around my shoulders. Then down my arm, coiling around it. Jessie's snake, Karma, had lifted herself up, and I leaned down and let her crawl up my other arm. Then she coiled around it and I slid into the music.

I held up my arms and undulated my torso, moving slowly in a circle. The crowd came together like one body holding its breath. Slowly, I lowered my arms and let the snakes crawl around my middle and down to coil around my thighs. Then, slowly, I unwound one of the snakes, stretched it between my hands, bent backward, and held it above my chest. I got lots of applause.

We brought in about eleven hundred dollars that Sunday with our afternoon and evening performances. Priam was ecstatic. Jessie took the opportunity to let him know he'd better keep me happy if he wanted to get any good out of me. And hinted strongly that if he wanted her around . . . She told him I would be earning money just doing the dancing. And that ought to satisfy him. People would hire me out for parties and special events, I was that good. So I figured my way was clear. I was getting close to eighteen, and I couldn't wait for the day. Only things happened different from what I expected.

"Don't get too comfortable," Priam warned me. "I got plans. Big plans, beyond your wildest dreams." That scared the bejeezus out of me, especially since I had no idea what he had in mind. "It's a secret," he said, "And if you tell anybody . . ."

"What am I supposed to tell?"

But I told Jessie anyway, and how scared I was. "I think I know what's going on in his brain," Jessie said. "I heard him talking to the new gals, and I'll bet they put a bee in his bonnet. Ventura City. Who knows, maybe you'd get some good experience, and if you got on there with the snakes, you could advance your career."

I didn't know if she was trying to reassure me, keep me from falling into despair. "You never know in this life, lovey. It could be the chance of a lifetime. Maybe I'll give a look there myself one of these days." She gave me a wink and a little pat on the shoulder.

But I wasn't convinced. If Priam was all for it, there had to be something wrong with it. I really wanted to take off—my eighteenth birthday was now only four months away. But I still had the Kid to worry about, because with him it would be harder to cover my tracks. So I had to wait. As long as I was under age, Priam could set the sheriff to tracking me down. And he'd do it, too. Jessie told me to be patient and not do anything to get me in trouble. So I held my breath, just waiting for an opportunity to strike out on my own.

IX.

Nevada has everything—desert and mountains, a big lake, Paradise Valley, and Black Rock Desert, and Goldfield, a piece of Death Valley, and right there in the toe of the state, Las Vegas. I wrote off to the chamber of commerce, and they sent their brochures to Jessie. I was a little worried, though, about what I'd be getting into on my own. Would anybody hire me? They had all kinds of talent they paid big bucks for in the clubs. And what went over big at the Kitty Kat might look pretty small potatoes up there with the glitter. If nothing better turned up, I thought maybe I could get on as a waitress in a bar somewhere until I got the lay of the land, then try to work my way in with the snakes. But how would I travel with them? Always questions.

Nevada was the shape of my dreams for the future. Nights before I dropped off to sleep, I'd dream over those pictures, and when I could snatch a moment I'd read over and over the descriptions of the big nightspots, till I had them all memorized. Then I'd try to think up ways of living in a big city, how I'd get around, what I could do for the Kid.

I figured I had a little space and time left, once we came back after Priam pushed us into making a disastrous trip to Ventura City. He hadn't been able to get that out of his head. So off we went. At least I was going there as entertainment. I can't tell you how awful the trip was, going through the mountains—the hairpin turns churned my stomach upside down and scared me witless. Anybody would be a nervous wreck with Priam driving. Forget the Kid throwing up. We had to stop.

"Clean that up," Priam said. He was all caught up when we finally made it.

Oh, there were lights and dazzle enough to pop your eyeballs, the place all ribboned with neon, ads moving up and down the sides of buildings—figures of can-can girls and strippers, whiskey bottles and balloons, monkeys swinging through the wires. Seemed like every street was lined with bars and nightclubs, hot spots with porn flicks, and gambling joints. Something for everybody—but not much for us.

Priam took me around to various clubs, but even when we could get in, there wasn't much interest, the managers having to listen to a spiel from a scruffy old windbag. We had to settle for a little hole-in-the-wall run by Happy Max, who talked out of one side of his mouth and did us the singular favor of trying me out for a week. I was there for less than a month, putting out for two shows every night.

Exhausting. In the end, they plucked our feathers but good. The contract Priam had signed was for fifty/fifty, but written in the fine print were deductions for advertising, insurance, and special effects and all that came to quite a chunk. Priam barely had enough to pay for the motel.

He stomped back to the club and exploded in front of Happy Max, who squinched up his face, furrowed his brow, narrowed his eyes to slits. A nod, a little gesture with his index finger, and two of his men, big guys, sauntered in and just stood there, one showing strong interest in his fingernails, the other smoking a small thin black cigar.

"All that trouble for next to nothing," Priam kept grumbling as we tackled the mountains again. But once we were back after that heart-stopping ride, he swaggered around like a winner and boasted. "A great thing just for the experience."

He'd got it into his head he was going to climb the golden ladder as an impresario. He spent a wad on an outfit—ruffled shirt with silver studs, coat with tails, black trousers with room for his belly, and top hat. He'd do something special with that old theater. Harvey, the owner, was happy to pick up some loose change renting the Coyote while he waited for a buyer. Priam had it in mind to show a little porn on Saturday and Sunday afternoons and let me do my act before the show. At first the attendance was pretty good, since the tickets were cheap.

But the real action was out at the Kitty Kat, where most everybody wanted to be. Priam, too. Liked to strut his stuff onstage in his outfit and make a big deal of Jessie and me and the strippers. Joking with the audience. Reacting to the snakes. He was in his element all right.

Since I figured I was safe for a while, I kept my working in the direction of my own dreams. Jessie talked Priam into giving me a percentage of the proceeds from the theater, so I could save up a bit more money.

A lot of scheming and dreaming. But I could have saved myself the trouble, as I watched it all go up in smoke. One afternoon after I'd shown my stuff at the theater and was sitting backstage, just relaxing over a soda and a copy of *Cosmopolitan* I'd borrowed from Tina, this guy barges in—nobody's done that before, except whoever was taking me and the snakes back to the house. But this guy shows up in a blaze of strong feeling and starts praising me to the skies.

"Young lady, I got to tell you, you are terrific." I figure him for some kind of masher and gave him a big cold shoulder.

"I mean it. I damn well mean it. Let lightning strike me if I don't." He was good-looking in a frantic, hard-driving kind of way. Well-muscled, but not fat. How could he be, with all the energy pouring out of him? And putting out his spiel, like he had to use up all the words in him so he could sock in new supply. "Let me introduce myself. Just call me Dusty. I'm head honcho for a big deal, the Carnival for the Gods. I want to have a little chat with you."

You couldn't stop him. I was gorgeous, Number One. He'd never seen anything like me. Yeah, sure.

"Look, Mister, I'm trying to drink my soda and read my magazine. I'm sure you've got lots of things to do."

But he wasn't going to be put off. His expression was all tightened up towards what he was aiming to pull off, face square and solid, body ready to move like a fireball.

"You gotta listen to me," he says. "Why sit here in this crumby fleabag when the sky's the limit? Miss Gorgeous, I've got my own show, and you'll be the star. I mean it, every cotton-picking word." He held out his arms. "Just let the lightning strike."

My head started spinning—I didn't know what to make of him, but he was making my head ache. I held up my hand.

"I'm not free," I told him, figuring that would end it. "I got obligations. And I got plans of my own."

"You just wait a little. What are these obligations and who am I going to have to talk to?"

I put my hands over my ears. "I can't listen anymore. You're heading up the wrong track. Now quit hassling me and go back to where you came from—or I'll call the cops."

"Okay, okay," he said with a wave of the hand. "I got the message."

He left me pretty rattled. I kept waiting for Priam to come for me, wondering what held him up. Pretty soon, I found out. Wish I'd known.

Dusty had found his way to the Kitty Kat, tracked down Priam across the road, and talked his way into some kind of deal. The two of them had decided my future without the blink of an eye, without a glance in my direction. And what was I? Just a piece of property changing hands. The Kid was coming with me—he was part of the deal—not because Dusty wanted him but because, finally, Priam could get him off his back.

And that was how the Kid and I came to the Carnival for the Gods—a whole new page of the story.

When Priam gave me the news, I told him, no way, I had plans of my own.

"Why I never saw such an ingrate," he exclaimed. "Here comes a real emperor-o-sario, ready to put your name in lights over there in Venttura City . . . Why any other girl with the sense God gave a grasshopper . . . And that's what I been dreaming of for you myself. Going down there and making us rich—only he's the one with the connections. And you, you're about to wreck the chance of a lifetime."

"I don't care about any of that," I cried. "I don't want to go off with some stranger I don't know anything about. And there's the Kid."

He got ugly then. "You listen to me," he said, stabbing my chest with his forefinger. "I finally got something back for all the grief I've been put to, and you're not going to screw it up. You do, and you'll be sorrier than you've ever been in your life. It's all done, signed and sealed."

Now here comes Dusty, all full of himself, smiling at me, making Mr. Nice. "Listen, girl, it's like I been telling you. You'll be a star. You'll sail up in a blaze of glory. If Dusty can't do it, nobody can."

That's what I was afraid of. Priam stood there in his triumph—he'd pulled off the best deal he could ask for. He had his gloat over glory—that look.

Trapped. Nowhere to run. Jessie wasn't there to help me, even if she wanted to. No one else I could think of going to—the sheriff and the police were in Priam's pocket.

It had taken a while for Priam to round up the Kid—had to wait till he got back from the arroyo wanting food. He had to gather up our clothes and convince the Kid to get into his truck. The raven was there on the Kid's shoulder. The Kid would never say how Priam got him to go. Priam wouldn't even let me go back to say goodbye to Jessie, to tell her I loved her, and Louise, and Alabama, Nellie, and the others.

"I'm not going to have a bunch of pussy cats caterwauling over you," he said. "Or trying to wangle something out of me. No, this deal is done."

And suddenly I knew, lost in my scheming and dreaming of getting away, that I'd been in a place where I'd been happy. Except for what had always been trying to drive me away. It was all I could do to keep from breaking out into a wail.

The day was nearly gone when we got Pajarito, a supply of frozen mice, the Kid, and me all stowed in Dusty's truck and took off down the highway. I was looking into a distance farther than any I'd ever known or imagined. Seemed like it could go on forever. Out of town a ways down the potholed blacktop, we slowed, then pulled into a space cut off from the road, and I saw a small group of trailers parked along a flat spot. I knew right then—knew in my bones—the show I'd be star of was at the bottom of the heap out there in the middle of nowhere.

Dusty started unloading our stuff from the truck, taking out the crates with the snakes—he'd actually taken one of Jessie's I had at the theater—the cage with the raven, the bag with my costumes, and clothes for me and the Kid. There wasn't a whole lot. The Kid and I just stood there holding onto our separate silences. The past was a piece of smoke rolling away into the desert with the tumbleweeds.

I was about to crumple into a heap. A rectangle of light appeared from the trailer near where we'd parked, and a woman stepped out. When she came up close, she could have been holding up a mirror to show me all I felt inside. Glum, trying to hold the lid down. I stood there chilled to the bone—the desert gets cold at night—and neither the Kid nor I had a decent jacket. I was hugging myself to keep off the cold.

And that was how I made my entrance into stardom at the Carnival for the Gods.

"This is Grace," Dusty said, "Amazing Grace. You ought to see what she can do." Everything he said sounded wrong coming from his mouth. Nothing I could claim as I stood there shivering. There was a little hitch to her shoulder, and she gave me a look like I'd stolen somebody else's claim that had no gold to it anyway. But then her face softened. Maybe she saw how cold I was. "This here's Alta," Dusty said, like she didn't matter one way or the other.

She looked from me to the Kid.

"C'mon inside," she said, beckoning us towards the door of the trailer. "You'll catch your death out here." The way she spoke to me nearly brought tears to my eyes. "You hungry?"

I was starved—I hadn't eaten all day—and I could tell the Kid was about to cave in. We followed her inside the trailer and stood there uncertainly: a new place, new air, new sensations. We were there in the middle of the strangeness. Alta pointed in the direction of the bathroom and first the Kid and then I went to wash up. The smell of what was in the big pot on the stove had already sent my stomach growling. I knew chili beans. We had our eyes on the spoon as Alta served out bowls of chili and a plate of crackers. Came a giant and a midget—Donovan, who filled up the place, and Curran, who seemed to resent that he didn't—and an ordinary-looking fellow named Billy, the greatest magician of them all, Donovan said, and also handy with a hammer and nails. He winked at me.

Then Dusty appeared.

Through the window I could see the dark closing up the day. While I watched Alta dishing things out, she looked up at me and our eyes met and held. And it seemed her future, maybe everybody's was as uncertain as mine.

Next morning Dusty announced we were heading over to the Seven Cities to try out luck in Ventura City. Right away. Priam had painted the golden dream inside his skull, and he was ready to cash in. Going to show me off, get the loot to put himself back among the living, and build up the great show he'd been dreaming of all these years.

I cringed. I'd been there. When I got a free moment, I tried to tell Alta how it was when Priam took over.

"I figured as much," was all she said. It was risky going to her like that . . .

"Look here, what's this Ventura City business?" Alta challenged Dusty in the midst of his bustling around. "What makes you think things are going to fall into our laps?" I could tell she was angry. "Grace has been there and she sure isn't keen on going there, and neither am I. It was a bust."

"What do you know about it? And what did that old fart know?" He stood with his arms akimbo, taking her on. "Nothing. A big fat nothing. Nor Grace neither." He just pushed both of us aside. "It's a big city, get it?—lots of nightclubs and tourists, okay? And what does that mean?"

He allowed a little space for an answer. Alta kept mum.

"Lots of people with loose change. Just burning holes in their pockets. And what does that promise, dammit?" He held his hands open, handing all that promise to her, the quiz contestant lacking brains. "A gold mine—that's what. I took the gamble—hocked everything. Yes, I know—you think I've sold you out from under. Well, just hang on. The future's standing there waiting. Can't you see? Can't you just see it?"

She'd been asked to see a lot of things—that I could tell—and had watched the flames go out. Painted smoke in all its colors. "It is your picnic." She bit her lip and stared straight at me. Maybe she was just seeing me as her next piece of trouble.

Things were pretty rocky between them the rest of the morning as everybody got themselves ready for travel, and the look I'd seen on her face hadn't gone away. Then at lunch Dusty reached over and patted her hand. "It's our big chance," he said, opening his arms to the future. "We can do it, Dream Girl."

Her expression softened, as her iciness melted away. He was asking her to believe in him. And somehow she had to do it in spite of all he must have dragged her through. What else was there for her to do? He'd won the round, at least for the time being.

X.

I never expected to be a sensation. But Dusty bought me costumes like you wouldn't believe. Gowns with feathers and sequins for my first appearance onstage, low cut, half cups, tight waisted, open at the midriff, draping to the floor or signing off just above the knees, sides slit, taken over by black tights with designs in them. A lacey black number; a see-through of cloudy blue; a red hot, dazzling flame-thrower with little flashing lights all over. Then the bodices—all colors with matching embroidered panties and gold tights. He must have spent a fortune, got himself in hock to the nines.

Alta could only hold her tongue—you could see in a glance just how pissed she was.

She had tried to show me the costumes, mostly hers, collected over the years from the time she was on the trapeze. She clung to them like they were her skin, pulling at reluctant zippers, giving attention to spots of wear. But Dusty pulled me aside and said, "Don't bother with any of that rubbish. Probably wouldn't fit anyway. We'll get you some eye-catchers."

I felt a disloyalty. Alta had treated us well, me and the Kid too, like we were just part of the family. Didn't seem to be put off by the wildness that he was, the gleam of hostility in his eyes. Just took us in.

I'd already taken a shine to Billy, who liked to joke around with me, and even Donovan, whose eye didn't go deeper than my skin and liked to linger on what was under my neckline.

Dusty had cozied up to me when we were traveling down to the Seven Cities—actually put his hand on my knee. But I shrugged it off like it had accidentally wandered off-limits and kept my eye on the road. Strictly business. I knew in my bones he was pretty frisky with the gals, and that he drew them like honey. Charm—he had the full supply. He was ready to flaunt all his assets, even though he was getting a bit of a paunch around the gut. And besides, I owed something to Alta.

I didn't have to worry about the midget. He kept his distance, looked at me like I was down there with the snakes, and whenever he spoke to me, he didn't look up. Skipping past breasts, navel, and crotch down to the feet. No eye contact. Pure avoidance. A deep disgust. Fine with me. It was one less male I had to fend off.

Anyway, first it was the costumes. Then it was publicity, getting me in the public eye. I hadn't known anything about that and even Priam had no idea of its power. Soon there were photos of me on every billboard, bulletin board, and telephone pole—my face and figure, my waist and arms snake entwined. They sent around a sound truck broadcasting my name, Grace the daredevil snake girl, who'll put your heart in your mouth and bewitch you with her power. They even flew up a plane that wrote AMAZING GRACE across the sky. I felt embarrassed as all get-out but all that hoopla brought the crowds, and the owner of the nightclub, A. P. Valdemar—"Just call me A.P., honey," he said, with a flash of his gold tooth. He strutted around with the kind of smirk that made me want to slap him.

"Listen," he said. "I've been in this business since before you were born, and I know how to pack them in thicker than lemmings."

"Ladie-e-s and Gentlemen, we now present the feature of the evening, Amazing Grace—and she is AMAZING. She'll take you places you've never been. And keep you hungering for more. An Amazing performance, folks. Just keep your eye on that little blue butterfly on her belly, and you'll take wings."

So there I was at The Olde Black Magic doing my act every night, working with the snakes, inventing new moves and rhythms and patterns to keep the act fresh and lively. All to keep the patrons coming. Oh, yes.

I'd start boldly, entering like a princess, with the music announcing my presence there to be admired. Applause for me in one of my stunning outfits. The glamour girl. Then fanfare fell away, the music slinking into silk, suggesting something like a hand moving towards a thigh—that old black magic has me in its spell—as the crowd paused over their highballs and filet mignons and gave me their eyeballs to take where I wanted them to go. Then I would shed the frills, doing a few moves as the music snaked along: sexy belly-dance music. I'd lift the snakes after they'd s-curved from the basket, and let them coil around me, then take up the movements into the dancing, till those sitting out there were really into it, their forks poised in midair, too fascinated to take a bite. I could feel the tension, the excitement crackling through like an electrical charge. Then the band would go into the finale—sax, clarinet, trumpet, drums, and piano going into a crescendo for the climax, as I took up a snake and put its head into my mouth. The crowd came together in a single gasp, whoop, roar, bellow, whatever hit the air. Then the applause—like a thunderclap. From the back that first time, I could hear Donovan's deep voice, "My God, oh my God!"

Suddenly there was a rain of money. Dropping and feathering down. It just came at me—silver dollars, dollar bills, fives, tens, twenties. One night, a hundred bucks just sailed towards me like a bird headed for my hand. And for a while, it happened every night—like people couldn't leave without emptying their pockets, bringing out their amazement and laying it at my feet. Tribute. I was a celebrity. People came up for my autograph. The girls back at the Kitty Kat would have been struck dumb.

Only Curran wasn't having any of it. A butterfly on my belly? Wiggling around with snakes. Yuck. When I put the snake's head in my mouth, he actually put his hands over his eyes. And at breakfast, while Donovan was going wild over my moxy, he could barely get down his soft-boiled egg. "Well, it's a living," I said. He glanced up at me, then, looked at me with a certain recognition and, for a moment, seemed almost humbled. But he had a heavy wad of disgust to get past.

Dusty was all full of himself, as might be expected. "See what I told you?" he said to Alta. "You wouldn't believe me. But there's life in the old hide yet. I knew we'd hit pay dirt."

"Well, you've got the goods, kiddo," Alta said, as she got up to do the dishes, putting her arm around my shoulder. "You've saved our bacon, that's for sure."

I was about to clear the table and help her with the cleanup, but Dusty put a restraining hand on my wrist. I was above all that. I shouldn't dirty my all-too-valuable hands.

"I don't care what you say. I don't like the looks of that hustler," Alta said, her back to us. "He looks like bad news to me, like he'd rape his grandmother in the garden if it would put a dime in his pocket."

Dusty rolled his eyes and pulled a face for the rest of us. "Oh shit, Alta—get real. He's a businessman, for Christ's sake. What d'you want? He makes dough off the old tits and ass routine and everything in between. And you know what? That's what people are made of—the old wiggle—all the way back to Adam and Eve. Just try and change that. Only Grace here has got class—she's in another category." His look of appreciation nearly turned me inside out. It was all too much, way too much.

"A.P.'s got smarts," Dusty went on. "He knows how to appeal to the public, not just put on a show, but put one over. People are lapping it up."

Alta turned to glare at him. "I thought you were a circus man," she said. "Carnival for the Gods—what we were supposed to be about—a great dream of beauty and daring."

The others had taken themselves off one by one. Maybe they saw another knock-down-drag-out was building and didn't want to be in the fallout. I itched to go out, myself, but Dusty had a point to prove and he held me there, his hand still over mine like we were on a date. I was supposed to be on his side, but it was all making me nervous. Like I was about to step into quicksand.

"So what do you want?" Dusty shot back at her. He jerked himself up out of the chair, pointed his finger at her as if he'd stab her with it. "You think I don't have my dreams." Then he was out the door.

For Alta it was an old story—you could tell that—how she'd gone along with the dance, adjusting to all the detours. She was muttering now. Only what if the dream you were so sure about—all or nothing—started to turn into a nightmare. It was a question. "I don't like it."

Meanwhile people were swarming in for the magic. Over the top. Made the Kitty Kat look like kindergarten. You walked into the flush of the fever. Red-flocked wallpaper and all kinds of doodads in silver and gold. At one side of the entrance was a towering figure on a pedestal, a glowing goddess in the buff, sea shells at her feet, and a big clock where her stomach should have been surrounded with diamonds. It tinkled out a tune: "If you got the money, honey, I got the time." Mirrors were strung along the walls, and when you looked in, you somehow saw another image of yourself, but changed dramatically, stripped naked, boobs and butt wiggling so you could see all the moving parts as you watched the other you jollying her crotch, or mooning you, looking over her shoulder, winking, smirking. I don't know what the guys saw when they looked into the mirrors. No doubt the same kind of things.

"I've got to hand it to you, A.P.," Dusty said, as he showed us around. "You sure know how to set the bait." A.P. made the gesture of counting bills.

"I see he's got two things on his mind," Alta said after the tour. "I doubt there's room for more."

"Get real," Dusty said. "It's our bread and butter."

"And when are we going to do circus?—we're getting rusty."

"We got to get to a starting place first, unless you want to start from broke," Dusty fired back. "And we got a ways to go."

"We've got more money than we've seen for years," Alta countered. "Why not get back in gear?" She may as well have been talking to herself.

We'd been treated to one of A.P.'s filet mignon dinners that night after my first great successes there, and when Alta got up to go to the Ladies, Dusty leaned over and patted me on the shoulder. "Make her jealous. Rub it in."

That startled me. As it was, I was worried she might think I was moving in on her territory. I wanted her on my side, I knew that much. I'd dropped down in her midst. She didn't owe me a crooked penny. But there were times she looked at me with a tenderness that made me want to cry.

I didn't have much time for the Kid, but Billy had taken him over, and the Kid stuck to him like pitch. They were up and out right after breakfast and gone most of the afternoon . The Kid didn't talk to anybody, but that was okay. Billy was the one for talking—one long monologue while they moved around the streets or rambled up into the hills. Slowly, taking their time. They didn't have anywhere to go, anything special to do, but by the time Billy came back, he had a whole picture to paint right before your eyes.

"Today we went to Paradise, didn't we, Kid?" Trying to take him into the conversation. "The Paradise Regained Club, with gambling and entertainment. Just passed by the doorway, mind you. But it was open to our two pairs of eyes, such was our curiosity, and we stood there gawking—it was a sight. Then a nice young fellow—I think he was in charge of cleanup—said, "Come on in and take a look around." And he turned on all the lights.

"Well, Paradise is quite a place when you regain it. Only better to never have lost it. Doesn't smack much of the original. The apples hanging from the trees are plastic lights on invisible wires hanging from the ceiling, all colors. Blues and reds and purples. And when they're all lit up, shining down on the upholstery, with all the silver and copper and brass decorations, it's like standing drunk in the middle of a pinball machine. Something to see all right. And there's a little pool in the middle, with big orange carp swimming through, for everything to reflect on, and some artificial grass around it, and a big green stuffed frog sitting there like it was ready to snatch a few flies out the air. And I reflected on it all and saw you needed another club alongside called 'Original Innocence,' and that would be harder to come by."

Well, he'd go on like that till Donovan, the first to leave, got up, stifling a yawn, and then Dusty and Curran. Alta and the Kid and me stuck around. The Kid took it all in like it was meat and drink, his eyes glued to Billy's face. I loved to listen to him spin his yarns, and I loved him for what he was doing for the Kid.

Then I'd get up to go to the room reserved for me at the motel and see to the snakes, feed them if they needed it, leaving them just a little hungry so they'd have the motive for movement, and listen to the radio and try not to think about being Amazing. One afternoon I startled Dusty by asking him to take me to the library. I filled out a card and checked out a couple of books called *The Scarlet Letter* and *Great Expectations* because I'd heard of them and they were supposed to be good. I got to read some before lunch, and I dreamed about going to school one day and how it would be. Sometimes afterwards I'd go out walking with Billy and the Kid.

There were streets where the big club owners and entertainers lived, houses out of adobe or stone, two or three floors high, a jeep or a landrover parked outside, or maybe a Cadillac or a Lincoln under a metal awning. The yards were big, with stones around a collection of cactuses, even roses. We wondered where they got the water. Usually there'd be a Mexican or two raking up the yard, trimming cedars, keeping things spiffy.

We'd walk out to where the sidewalks ended and the streets turned to dirt, full of ruts, and the adobes had maybe one room and a kitchen, the doorway open and a gaggle of kids, mostly barefoot, and a bunch of dogs, all sizes and shapes, playing outside. The huts were pretty ramshackle, with their rusty-looking cars in front or in the drive. They all had TV antennas on the roofs. Reminded me of what I'd left behind. I can't say I wanted to go back to that, but a sudden confusion came over me about where I'd found myself. I felt a lump in my throat. The gals at the Kitty Kat had been my family, and I wasn't used to the new one yet. My name felt like a sticker without any glue.

All the time we were meandering Billy was going on with his spiel. "Now they got all that entertainment along the gulch—glitter and gauze—but they could do with a little magic out here." And one morning when we passed a playground, he gathered all the kids around him and started blowing up balloons and twisting them into the shapes of dogs and cats and horses and birds and sailing them out to the kids, who caught them, giggling and crying out. "Do one for me. Para mi."

Things went on like that for several weeks, till I was getting pretty used up performing every night. Then A.P. kept me for just one show midweek and the rest for weekends. Dusty had been trying to get places for Curran and Donovan to do a comedy act and for Billy to do his magic show. They managed a few gigs around town, just to keep their hands in and pick up a little change. But they weren't a hot item, and the pickings were pretty thin. A lot of people poured through the city, out for a screaming good time, but you could keep an act going for only so long. You had to convince folks they were getting the latest and the greatest, the hottest, the most immodest, the most thrilling thing on the billboards. Name and fame—that was the ticket, the stairway to the stars. I sensed I'd had my big moment and the novelty had worn off. I was hoping we could move on. Alta had been nagging in that direction. But not yet.

One Saturday night after the act was over, Dusty had everybody gather at the club—he had an important announcement for us. A.P. himself was on hand with his waiter pouring out champagne. We had something to drink to. "Our little star is going to do a film." A.P. was all smiles, refilling everybody's glasses. "Let's drink to our super-star." Dusty started applauding.

I was flabbergasted. A film. A.P. was a little thin on details. "We're putting together a crew right now, some of the best in the industry. And hiring the actors. It's still in the works," he said, "but we're gonna do it." He slammed his fist into his hand. "A stunner like Grace is all you need."

"What is this film anyway?" Alta wanted to know, when she got Dusty cornered at breakfast. "Where's it going to happen? You read the script, met the crew?"

"Hold on, hold on." Dusty said. "They're putting on the finishing touches right now. And the actors are coming down from Hollywood this week. We'll have the contracts in a couple of days."

"And you're already at the center of this without letting us know what we're getting into. You must be out of your mind."

"Listen," Dusty said, "These things take time. It's a big deal."

Before we knew it, the camera crew and actors were in town, and I was supposed to go out later that week for some of the preliminary scenes. They were coming by to show me where they were setting things up, just to introduce me, take me through, and show me what they wanted.

"Damn it, give me a few details," Alta insisted at breakfast, after we got the news.

"Okay, it's a love story—lots of sex."

"Oh, great. A porn film, you mean. That's what it sounds like to me."

"Hold on—you're jumping to conclusions. Lots of films have got sex all over the place. So what—if it's got razzle-dazzle."

"Okay—so go on."

"Well, there's a shipwreck. Grace hitches on to a plank and swims to an island."

"In the middle of this desert," Alta says. "What is this, a fantasy?"

"Hell, they made a jungle for Tarzan right in the middle of L.A. You can even see the telephone wires in the flick. They can do anything. You wanted to know the plot, didn't you? Well, keep your pants on and listen." He was breathing hard, at the point of exasperation. Alta wasn't far behind.

"She's alone, and then a man appears and—it's—it's love at first sight."

"Really original," Alta says.

"Only there's three other guys,"

"And they all want a piece of her. Holy shit."

Dusty waved her off. "Only there's a tiger . . ."

"What does he do—eat her alive?"

"Dammit, Alta. Sam's going to make some money off this. And they'll use Lila."

"The elephant too. It sounds pretty fishy to me. Where's the script?"

They were hard at it—like watching a tennis match. I sat there like a stump, not knowing what to say. Like everything else, it all was going to be decided for me.

"They're going to be mostly improv," Dusty said. He always had an answer.

"It sounds like a goddamn free-for-all. And it's happening two days from now? Why the big rush? When's Grace supposed to practice, memorize her lines?"

"Listen, they know what they're doing. Lots of experience. They'll let her know what she's supposed to do."

"I want to be on hand," Alta said. "I'm wardrobe mistress, remember."

"Strictly off-limits," Dusty said, "No interference till they get it shot and in the can. Not even me."

Before they got into the fight Alta was heading towards, Dusty gave her a wave of impatience, turned on his heel, and was off to the city to close the deal.

The first day of the filming, Dusty took me down to the nightclub and, despite what he'd said to Alta, he stayed around for the action. Cameraman, director, and actors were on hand, the actors a bunch of hunks that kept giving me the eye.

The tables alongside the pool had been moved aside and the fake palm trees moved to an island fashioned out of artificial turf set on an anchored float with a few rocks brought in for a realistic touch. There was a take with me swimming to the island. Struggling with exhaustion, and clinging to a rock in my torn chemise and panties, half dead, barely able to hang on. In comes the big hero, the tall-dark-handsome type. Just in time to keep me from sinking back into the sea. He revives me—We take a long look at one another and cling together and kiss. The love-at-first-sight bit. Passion.

The director, a small gray-faced guy with a tic that knits his face into odd expressions, wants to have my new love take me from behind, but I put up a fuss. He and A.P., who is all tuned into the action, have a brief confabulation. We agree to simulate the scene.

Then one by one, three big-muscle types show up, wanting a piece of the action and good times for all. Me giving one of them a head job and making with golden palms for the other two. All at once. "You gotta have a sense of rhythm all right," A.P. says, full of appreciation.

So I figure, what the hell, and throw myself into it, flirting with the guys, joking and wisecracking. I can't say I didn't enjoy that part of it. Not anything I'd have chosen. Even though I came out okay. They told me I was terrific, a natural. *For what?* I thought. For doing it for money. And though I didn't understand it then, I was afraid of them.

Alta was pissed as all get-out. She wanted everything to end right there.

"Look," she said, when Dusty had laid out the pile on the kitchen table, "the money' s rolled into our laps. We've got the bankroll you wanted. Let's get the hell out while the getting's good." She gathered it up immediately and put it in a drawer.

"What are you talking about?" Dusty waved a contract in front of her nose and said he wasn't backing down—Priam said Grace could do anything—and that was that. He'd paid out good money, a damn sight of it, too. And she, Alta, could go to hell. She told him get out before she killed him.

He was gone most of the evening, and she wasn't speaking to him when he came back. He was jotting things down on paper, figuring things all morning.

"I don't like any of this," she said to Billy after she went to tell him to come over for lunch, but she was really talking to Dusty.

"What is in the contract? I'll bet he hasn't even read it."

The Kid and I weren't saying anything. Donovan and Curran were gone for the day—Donovan for a tour of the massage parlors, Curran to buy a new suit. And Dusty was primed.

Without a word Dusty went to the refrigerator, pulled out some ham, and made himself a sandwich. He didn't look at her while she tended to the rest of us—you could tell he was all in his head, tuning everybody out.

"Can't you see what's happening to us?" Alta said, almost pleading. "What we've lost . . ."

"Gotta go," Dusty said, hustling out. She had only Billy to turn to. "Donovan's still enjoying himself, the old rogue, but Curran's had it up to here."

"I'm with you, Dream Girl."

"Buttonhole Dusty, will you?"

Billy shook his head. "Wouldn't do any good. There's that agreement. The money he got dazzled him. Got him all excited, all his brags going. 'It's Carnival for the Gods, chum—that's what we're meant to be. New acts, new talent.' He's got the picture in his head. There's no talking to him."

"Yeah, I know."

The crew was supposed to do shots of the animals and me that afternoon. But here comes A.P. himself with the director and the big hero right in the middle of lunch, wanting me then and there. Something had balled things up with the tiger that morning, and they wanted to cut out that scene and do the next scene just with me. They hadn't told me yet what that was all about.

The rest of the crew was on the lot. "We got a great location," A.P. said, "not too far from town—everything we need."

"So where is this place?" Alta demanded.

A.P. frowned into some quick thinking and said, "Just past Las Margaritas. Small building on the left-hand side. Used to be a tattoo place there. Well, gang, we better get going. Got a heavy schedule today."

I got to sit in front with A.P., him breathing heavy at my side. He was wearing some kind of cologne or aftershave that nearly made me puke, it was so sweet at first but with something underneath like rancid bacon. I stared out the window without seeing anything, while he kept talking, pointing things out, all the spots where three drunks had missed the road and landed in the gulch. "Happens all the time," he said with a chuckle. "I was there for one of them. Caused a lot of excitement.

"Poor bastard was only half killed—the other half wasn't going to do him much good."

Then he said, "You know, you get everybody hot just watching you go through your moves. What d'you think about that?

"I'm just doing what you and Dusty want," I said. "The rest is none of my business."

"But just think about it," he says. "Everybody getting a little thrill just because of you. The snakes, too, but this is dynamite."

I shrugged.

"And it's the greatest thing in the world," the director said from behind. "And you're giving something unique. That's why we're making this film. Because on film you're immortal."

"It's Dusty's idea," I said. They were making my nerves go haywire. Then I saw where we were going. It wasn't anywhere near town. We went past a big junkyard and a garbage dump, old tires and refrigerators and metal and rubbish all piled up.

"Where are we going?" I said, my head throbbing. "I thought you had a studio."

"We'll be there in a heartbeat," A.P. said, putting his hand over mine. "Just hold your horses."

But inside me, sirens were going off. When the car slowed to turn into a washed-out stretch that had no resemblance to a road, I opened the door, threw myself out, halfway fell to the ground, leaped up, and bolted. It was rocky and full of cactus and mesquite, yucca trees and sagebrush. Sharp needles and burrs tore at me as I tried to run. I heard the car jolt to a stop and car doors slam all around.

"Go after her," A.P. yelled. "Son of a bitch. We should have tied her up."

I didn't know where to run. The trees were mostly scrub cedar and juniper, nothing to climb or hide in. I headed towards a canyon and worked my way down into it, then up a slope on the other side, trying to find a place to hide somewhere in the rocks. A hunted animal running, hollowed out with a fear that took up all the space that I was. I ran without rhyme or reason, past a great rock into trees that snagged and grabbed at me. Almost falling, then regaining balance to run again, chest hurting for breath. Where to look, what to do. I dodged and bolted one way and another, then finally panting, a stitch in my side, I squeezed in between two rocks, hunkered down, tried to catch my breath, get calm enough to listen. At first, only the throbbing of my heart was in my ears. I just kept to my place, hoping the afternoon would leak into twilight and then darkness that would cover me.

They were breaking through the brush. I squeezed down as much as I could and prayed for escape. Then minutes later, they pounced on me. Dragged me out of my hiding place, kicking and screaming. They were too many for me. They captured my hands, my arms, pushed me down to the ground and shoved a jacket over my nose and mouth. I fought until I gave way, though I knew they were carrying me through the bush and brush. I was lying flat on something hard, a rock maybe like the big flat one I'd run past. My hands were tied behind my back, my legs pulled apart. A piece of metal shaped like a rocket glinted a little above me, not far from my feet.

"Give it all you got," someone yelled.

I closed my eyes and tried to leave my body. Then suddenly, there were yells all around me, running feet. A volley of stones.

"Kill them," I heard. "Kill them." More rocks flew. Familiar voices but strange, too. Harsh and shrill. I didn't know for sure till afterwards.

Billy and the Kid with him, with his deadly aim. At my side, lifting me, the Kid protecting the rear with more stones. The rest is a darkness.

XI.

After I came to, I had no idea where I was. Still in a darkness that boiled around me. Then as the memory of what had happened began to seep through and chain me to a horror, I couldn't stop shaking—not for a long time. Down there in a pit. The pain in my body pulsed with the pain in my mind until I thought I'd leap out of my skin. Just the thought of what those creeps wanted out of me! A moment's sensation before throwing me on the garbage heap. A film star all right, in a continually running nightmare. And when would it stop?

No, you didn't die. But there's a death all the same. Poor girl. I am here, walking beside you. Don't worry, little one. I am patient. I can take my time. You have felt only a touch. A chill—I know.

Alta was in a state. "I knew it, I just knew it."

She kept fuming as she bathed my feet and hands and smoothed on a soothing lotion, honeying me, trying to give comfort. I was limp in her hands, a jellyfish. I wanted to stop my ears and dive into silence. "When that lowdown . . ." she couldn't find the word—"shows up, I'll strangle him. I swear I will." I couldn't even care.

She did what she could for me, then put me to bed and sat by me holding my hand like I was a little kid. I could sense the jangle of her nerves, the energy of her anger. I wanted to turn away from her, just lie there in darkness and blank out, but there was something I had to let in—her feeling for me. It shone in her eyes and her touch and her face was softened by it. It made me teary-eyed, just knowing. But I was still chilled to the bone, still caught in the awfulness. If I let myself cry, I'd have split in two.

"Honey, you just relax, try to get a little shut-eye." I lay awake staring-eyed, thinking I'd never sleep again. Then I was gone, like I'd fallen down a well.

Dusty didn't show up. I was half awake a time or two and could hear Alta's hoarse whisper.

"Where can he be?—the bastard." She was all for pulling out right then, leaving Dusty to fend for himself.

"Hold on, Dream Girl," Billy kept saying. Then as the night wore on, she was all in a fever about what might have happened to him. I'd woken up and was lying there pretending to be asleep—I was aching all over, one big bruise—scrapes and scratches all over.

"I'll go see what I can find out," Billy said.

"Oh, Billy—be careful, Billy." Now she had three of us to worry about. Fortunately, her worry had sent Billy and the Kid out after me.

After searching half the night through the city, Billy finally found Dusty unconscious in an alley, beaten half to death. Fractured skull, broken ribs, broken arm, knees in bad shape. A mess. If Billy hadn't found him when he did, he'd have been dead. If he'd had any money on him, it was gone. Billy managed to call an ambulance and early that morning was back to tell the news. We caravanned outside the city, parked ourselves on a road to an abandoned silver mine, hoping we would escape notice.

Billy took charge, going into the city for food to keep us going, visiting Dusty in the hospital. We tried not to speak about our fears. Alta's was that Valdemar and his hoods would come after us.

"I'll bet they've got the police in their pockets. That kind usually does."

And who were we?—just a ragtag outfit with nobody to call to our side. They could find something to pin on us quick as swatting flies, so picayune you could find a joke in it, like not having the right license or parking in the wrong spot. But maybe we weren't worth their trouble. Maybe they'd gotten in trouble at some point themselves. Who knows?

We waited till Dusty was patched together in reasonable shape to travel. It took a while. All of us were eager as hell to get out of Ventura City. We needed a place where Dusty could convalesce and the rest of us could feel human again. The elephant was gone; heaven knows what had happened to her or the tiger. We couldn't take the risk of trying to find out. Sam, the trainer, remained behind to search for them. We packed up and went limping on our way, a bunch of casualties. You couldn't imagine a sorrier lot. No idea where we were going. There were other cities, six of them we didn't know anything about. I had the sinking feeling that each might be worse than the one before. Though it seemed like Ventura City qualified for the pits. We were all pretty glum, not just about what had happened but what might be in store.

It seemed like we'd thrown away all our chances and would spend forever bumping along winding rutted roads that took us to the inside of nowhere—only to get lost in it. Which we did the very first night out.

Lost in fog thicker than spit. Bumped right into the middle of the opaque with no way to go on. A big nothing was all you could see—except for a weak little gauze of light from the blurred moon overhead. When you looked out the window, you felt like the fog would suck you in, suck you down into some forever hole.

"Sure feels like home," Donovan said, after we came to a halt and stood around like a flock of ghosts.

"Seems like you could take just one step and fall off a cliff," Curran said. "Gives me the weemies. You don't dare take a step."

"At least in Ventura City you could see the gulch you'd be landing in," Donovan added. For once they agreed on something.

"Something's down there," Billy said, straining his eyes. "Like columns. Looks kinda like ruins."

"Your eyes are sharper than a ferret's," Curran said.

"Ruins? Good show. Throw out a guess in any direction," Donovan said, "and it'll be the same thing as being right. Right?"

"May as well tuck down till morning," Billy said philosophically, "till we can see where we're going. Not as if we know exactly where we are . . ."

"When have we ever known that?" Alta said.

Curran simply scowled.

It was the reverse, Billy said, of everything he knew. He was a now-you-see-it now-you-don't man. "The usual trick of illusion turned inside out. Now you don't see it, and if you ever do . . ."

"Okay, you bunch of cynics," Alta said. "Let's bed down for the night."

But it was hard to sleep, as if you were being worked on by mysterious powers—whether for good or ill, it was hard to say. It was strange the way things were beginning to work on me. Mysterious, that place. It seemed to work into my dreams, as though I'd been set wandering towards another life, partly buried, with certain glimpses . . . Of what, I didn't know.

When morning came, we saw where we'd landed and were just as mystified as we'd been the night before. And there it was: an ancient city fallen in ruins. Temples, what was left of them, with the columns Billy had spotted through the fog. And something strange farther on. We stood gaping at it in the daylight, and to our surprise, here comes Billy, with Curran in tow. He'd had a night of it.

"Well, what do you know?" Alta said. "Here come the explorers. What were you two doing down there?"

"Taking a leak," Donovan suggested.

To our surprise and his consternation, Curran had had an adventure he hadn't counted on. He'd been lying wide-wake while everybody else was trying to sleep, lying there till he got the fidgets. There was Donovan sawing away, he told us, grunting and calling out—usually the names of women he'd tried to sweeten up. Donovan winced. "I wanted to punch him—" Curran said.

"Only you couldn't reach up high enough," Donovan taunted him.

"Couldn't stand it any longer," Curran said. So he got up and went out. The fog hadn't completely dispersed, but the moon was brighter. He figured he could wander through whatever was down there and wait for sun-up, if there was going to be a sun. He grabbed a flashlight and went by himself into whatever was waiting. Must have been desperate to get through the night. Can't imagine him being that curious.

"So what was it like?" I wanted to know.

"Don't even ask," Curran said. "You don't want any part of it. See those stone figures—there's where I spent some of the worst hours of my life."

"Sort of a garden—looks like," Donovan said.

"Obscene," Curran said. "Gives me the willies just thinking about it. What sort of people lived there?" It was an accusation. "Like they wanted to make a prison for each other—out of their lust."

"Venus is pretty strong stuff," Donovan said, giving him a little punch—"for those who can take it."

"You oughta know, big boy," Curran said. "You wrap your mind around her often enough. Your fantasies would probably . . ."

"We gonna stand here all day practicing insults?" Alta said. "We need to get moving."

But not till Curran told how he'd gotten turned around in the fog and the dark and spent the night circling back to the same spot over and over, till he could hardly lift a foot. He'd called till he was hoarse.

Finally Billy heard him. "Hardly sun-up," he said. "Didn't know where the voice was coming from—it sounded so far away."

He'd wandered down in what seemed to be the right direction and waited for Curran to clamber over piles of stone to reach him.

"Then I saw the most amazing thing," Billy said in a rush of words. "Off to the side. A goldfish pond—with fish in it—and then . . ."

"Holy shit—a fishpond?" Donovan interrupted. "A bunch of ancient carp? Live or dead? Mummies?"

"No, listen."

I'd never seen him so excited. "It was a beautiful pond," he said. "Like a dream, sparkling. All green and gold. Fish just circling around. Orange and white and black and gold. Wish you all could've seen it. And when you looked into the water, there was a city down below, right at the bottom of the pond. Can you believe it?"

"No, frankly," Curran said. "You high on something?"

"But it was real, I swear it—only magic. Just imagine—buildings all in marble, all colors. Arches. Gardens with shrubbery and flowers—every color, I tell you. Only it was like you could see through them, to a light behind them. And there I was, just watching it open up before my eyes."

"Yeah," Curran said, "Yeah."

"I yelled for him to come quick. But the spell lasted only for a moment." Billy sighed. "We're back to what I know," Billy said. "Now you see it, now you don't. I guess that's my only territory."

I wanted to believe there was something there, something you could take in, that you'd want to remember and believe in, that you could find in the world and keep like a precious stone. Oh, I wanted it something fierce.

"I had one of the worst nightmares of my life," Donovan said, "if anybody's interested."

"Maybe we're all crazy," Alta concluded, "only some of us are crazier than others." And she went off to cook breakfast.

I hadn't seen the Kid all morning, and I was wondering where he'd got to. I slipped off while the others were still yammering. Curran was daring Donovan to go down there, and Billy was all for trying for another look into the fishpond. I wanted to look at the temple.

Not everything was in ruins. It took a little doing to get down there. The temple stood a little apart, a group of figures beyond it, maybe the sculptures that had aroused Curran's disgust. I stood for a moment in front of the temple, wondering if I should enter. I didn't know what I'd find there, but when I went up the steps and walked inside, a goddess was standing on a pedestal. Tall, awesome, with what looked like many breasts. And on the drapery of her garment were lions and bulls, birds and plants, and even a fly. It could have been all the creatures in the world. Maybe they belonged to her. Or came out of her. I made a little bow.

I could see a little sheen of water through the columns, beyond a pile of stones, maybe Billy's pond. Looked like it would take some climbing to get to it. I saw the Kid poking a stick into it.

"Hey," I yelled. "What's there?" He didn't answer but scrambled up over the fallen columns like somebody was after him and disappeared.

Had he seen anything? I couldn't leave without trying for it. So I left the temple and found an opening farther on and wandered into a series of paths that took me one way, then another. Really confusing, a maze. Taking me into little grottoes and byways with carved friezes and stone figures. Odd things. A naked woman, full of laughter, astride a donkey, leaning forward to hold her hands over its eyes. And where was it taking her? An old man trying to hold the feet of a bird that had landed on his head, flapping its wings. I was startled to see it had a human face, mouth opened in a cry, but whether of pain or triumph I couldn't tell. Other sculptures: youths and maidens chasing one another, some of the figures with raised fists, fierce, whips in their hands. When you looked at the figures they grabbed hold of you, possessed you with a kind of fascination, till your blood got all riled up. And you didn't know what to do.

Come join us. Get in the flow. You know the lowdown, how to flaunt your stuff. They taught you that, and you got good at it. A real pro. Dancing in and out of men's desires . Flirting the moola out of their pockets into yours as they got all hot and bothered. You're a woman, aren't you?

Whose voice was in it my ear? I couldn't stand it. I started backing away and nearly fell over a long round stone, curved into a hood at the end. It had fallen from a pedestal onto the ground. Seems like everybody had the same thing in mind—one way or another. Whenever I turned around, something boiled up from the darkness, and I'd see myself dancing at the Olde Black Magic, then out on the rock waiting to be sacrificed.

Finally I managed to get to the fishpond, but I couldn't make anything out, either because of the green scum on the surface—algae, I guess—or because the light was wrong. Seemed like I'd been dealt out of the game.

Oh, Billy! I cried to myself. *Was what you saw only for you?*

Alta was hollering for everybody to come to breakfast before it got cold. She'd taken care of Dusty first, had to feed him with a spoon. I worked my way up the slope. She'd set up a card table outside, and we all helped ourselves to scrambled eggs and bread and butter. And lots of coffee.

Afterwards Billy sat consulting a map, and everybody stood around offering their own version of where we were or weren't. Curran was so convinced he was right, he got red in the face, trying to convince the rest, Donovan gigging him all the way. The sites of the cities were marked with circles, but the map gave no indication of how far apart they were. Just little circles with marks around them. When you looked around you, the land fell away for miles. Empty but for the prickly pear and sage and jimson weed. Except for the ruins. We'd be running out of food and water if we didn't find something soon. The crows were on the lookout. A noisy lot of them skimmed back and forth over the stones and fallen columns. Waiting for a feast.

XII.

It took a while before we could see that the land was rising. We'd blundered our way along through a dry flat rocky landscape, with cactus here and there, some scrubby cedars, a few Joshua trees, and sage. Miles and miles. Then we spotted low hills in the distance, a hint of green. The vegetation was less harsh.

Alta let out a little cheer. "We're coming to something," she announced. "I can feel it—there's a change in the air."

I felt it too. You could breathe easier. Not so much dust.

We came to a crossroads on the narrow road, with a couple of signs too weathered to read. One had the letters "Tir . . ." The rest was rubbed out. The other was a big half-rusted sign that somebody had blasted full of bullet holes. We could read "At . . ." with an "a" at the end.

We stopped and looked at the map again. Circles but no names. Confusion at the crossroads. Should we turn left or right or just keep on going? The road ahead, though it was packed down like corrugated cardboard, had some recent tire marks. Billy thought he saw a sign a little way in the distance. We decided to go straight on. We trusted Billy's eyes.

"Old Town," we read, when we came up to the second sign. A real place. Then trees, the hint of water. Green hills—a river.

"Praise be!" Alta said. "Signs of life."

We passed a large open meadow with some black cattle, farther on, fields with horses, then a farm with dairy cattle. Farmhouses appeared, and we spotted a man with a cart full of tomatoes, squash, and melons. Then smaller houses with vegetable gardens. Rounding a curve near the river—slow going with the trailers, we found a boat landing set about with picnic tables and a fire pit in the middle. We paused.

Billy went in to see about parking the trailers—it looked to be the most likely spot. A couple of young guys ready to launch a boat helped us park them.

"You circus folks?" they said.

"That's right," we told them.

"Just what this town needs—some new entertainment. Glad to see you. Keep on going. Just around the bend. Hope you'll put on a show for us."

"That'll be the day," Alta said in a low voice to no one in particular.

The main street was lined with cottonwoods, old trees with big furrowed trunks like they'd been around since Methuselah. Our trailers would have blocked things up.

"Not exactly a city," Donovan commented as we came along a stretch of pavement with a long metal shed that opened into a garage. A couple of mechanics were at work on a battered truck. They paused to watch us pass, a bunch of unlikely strangers. On a sudden impulse, Curran leapt up into Donovan's arms. We all stood there laughing.

"I'll be damned," one of the men said. "When's the show?"

We walked on past a general store—feed and seed and you-name-it; past a carpenter's workplace; past an herbalist's shop, a hardware store, a shop with stationery and art supplies; past a coffee shop with tables out in front, men, women, and kids sitting out in the sunshine. We caused some little stir and commotion. We were used to that. A market with stands of fruits and vegetables at the front drew my eye.

"We'll have to stop there," Alta said. "I'm ready for some real food for a change."

"How about a nice thick filet mignon," Donovan said. "You can keep the carrots and broccoli. I think I could eat half a cow."

He knew eating all right. I'd seen him pack away a meal that would have kept me fed for a week. Three shrimp cocktails for starters, a huge sirloin, two or three ears of corn, a big salad with lots of tomatoes and cucumbers—ending with a great mound of German chocolate cake and three scoops of ice cream. He would lean back with a sigh of content: he was happy—for a while.

We came to the square, with the town hall, a small white building with the mayor's office; a neat little park in the center with bright flower beds, red and yellow, blue and purple. Just opposite stood the

Hotel Acropolis, with a drawing of the Parthenon, so Billy told me, below the letters on the sign. It had been around for a while, you could tell—maybe as old as the cottonwoods—the boards had all gone silvery gray. The rooms had little wrought-iron balconies and the shutters and door were a turquoise blue that looked like they'd borrowed the color from the sky. Alongside was a garden filled with flowers and vegetables, stones set in and around the beds. A big garden that extended from the side of the hotel to the back and filled most of the block behind. Reds and yellows, pinks and lavenders, whites and blues. All the colors.

We paused to take it in.

"That's Rina's garden," a passerby, an old man leaning on a cane, told us. We all stood admiring it. A woman with a blue-and-green scarf knotted around her white hair stood up, trowel in hand, from where she'd been working.

"And that's Rina," he said, giving her a wave. "In her nineties and still out there every day. Everybody knows her, goes to buy her herbs and flowers. See this head of hair—she cured me of going bald, She's a whizz."

We admired the results.

"Maybe she can do something for you, champ?" Donovan offered. Curran gave him a raspberry.

I looked at Alta, paying no heed to the rest of us, her eyes fixed on the garden.

The hotel was the real center of the town, everything else radiated from it. With two stories and an attic, it was taller than any other building on the street. Not far beyond the shops and houses, the town petered out—some few sheds and a couple of warehouses located on past where the pavement ended and the land opened into pasture. Other shops were on the backstreet. Nothing fancy, but nothing tumbledown either. The sign on the front of the hotel said, "Welcome," and that was all Alta needed.

"We're staying right here," she said, about to head for the door.

"Not in the trailers?" Curran said.

"Nope—we got the money, and we're going to do it."

I could have spent the rest of my life there, if it hadn't become the place I wanted most to flee from—a place even worse than Ventura City or where I grew up for all that happened there. Even now just thinking about it makes me cry. For all we had and what we lost—for all that seemed possible then.

It was a place for people like us, though we didn't know that when we came. Before we found we could belong there. Not a big place. A couple of thousand maybe, of people who'd wandered there out of their various desires and discontents. To get away from the century's noise and hurly-burly and grow their own food and plant flowers and raise their kids in a place where they could roam around and explore field and farm—live without too much junk. With friends and neighbors to turn to if they needed help or companionship.

The hotel, built when the town was first settled, had been run by the Triandophylos family ever since. It was more than just a place for wayfarers, some of which stayed in the town, while others traveled on—though they sometimes had a change of heart and came back to settle there. The hotel set the tone for the town—the center for news and happenings, plans and projects. People came to eat in the restaurant and gather in the bar for music and talk during the evenings. Kids played around on the swing sets and slides in the back. The teenagers had their own untamed spot, where they hung out and played their own music.

The present owners continued the tradition of hospitality, which was their pride. Elena did the cooking and cleaning; her husband, Alexos, kept things in repair and did the books; and their son, Leftheris, who welcomed guests and assigned their rooms, did everything to keep the place going. They were busy from daylight till late at night. Not to forget Rina and her garden. Anyone who needed help could come to them—and frequently did. At Christmas and Easter, they threw open the doors, opened up the great ballroom, and held a great celebration. People told me all about it. The whole town joined in, planning and building sets and floats, and sewing costumes for weeks in advance. There were parades and plays and pilgrimages with kids and animals, as well as grownups. Then everybody came to the hotel to join in eating the turkeys and roast meat and all the dishes the townsfolk had been preparing for days—drinking, dancing, and celebrating.

The inhabitants of the town had come from everywhere and done everything. They enjoyed the variety, though they had their own oddities in their midst. A former Olympics skater who drank his pork chops from a bottle and reeled around the streets, sometimes aiming a stream of cuss words or threats at somebody he mistook for the phantom in his head—but who, in his sober moments, was an expert carpenter and helped repair houses around town. A painter who did portraits of Lincoln from the Lincoln-head penny and tried to give them to the library. A former musical comedy star, who made candies out of honey in the shapes of dragons and butterflies. A recluse, who loved cats and kept over twenty of them and painted their portraits. There seemed to be room for everybody. Even us.

Once we got settled, we skipped off in our separate directions. Seemed like we'd had our fill of each other's company for a while and needed a break. When Dusty could get around again and didn't need waiting on, then Alta seemed happy to get shut of him, and be off on her own. She sat on the verandah drinking coffee or lemonade and reading magazines and doing crossword puzzles in a book she bought at the stationery store. When she got bored with that, she took herself over to the café, where she got acquainted with some of the locals and had long heart-to-hearts with a beautician named Beulah Murphy, who ran a hair salon. She gave Alta a facial and a perm that ended in an elaborate hairdo. Alta was pleased with herself for at least a week.

"Took ten years off me, I swear." She did look good. Seemed like a heavy weight was lifting from her shoulders, and she was letting go of an old ache.

She even got into mah-jongg for a little while with some of the older women, but that was going too far.

"I'm getting too damned civilized," she said. "And if I don't quit I'll lose my old sass."

Dusty was hardly out of bed before noon and stayed up till all hours, hanging out at the hotel bar, where there was generally a crowd, usually music, and a lot of palaver. He'd found himself a buddy, Captain Valor, broad-shouldered, paunchy, filled to the brim with army stories and bawdy songs, who spent his nights reliving his various bivouacs and heroic exploits. Dusty had stories of his own to match. They kept up a high-pitched battle to see who could get in the next word, each trying to collect a larger audience than the other, till finally, when those around them had had enough and only the two of them were still at it, they got happy or soppy.

They boozed it up together with great gusto, cackling over jokes, drinking till they could hardly stand. Then they parted from one another like the lords they were drunk as—swearing to remain blood brothers—and Dusty staggered off to bed.

The Kid did a good deal of roaming on his own. The closed-off parts of the hotel fascinated him, particularly one room where an artist had spent his last years. The walls downstairs were all decorated with his paintings, and his paints and brushes were kept just as he'd left them in the room upstairs where he worked. The Kid would plant himself in front of the paintings in the dining room, going from one to the other—till Elena asked him if he wanted to go up and look at the painter's room. For a second, the Kid looked like he'd just been offered a hundred dollar bill, then closed up like a clam. Billy and I went up with him.

The Kid didn't give anything away, but you could tell he was studying everything around him. I was about to look at some sketches in a book, but the Kid got to it first. Elena said he could turn the pages if he was real careful. I stood looking over his shoulder at the faces that seemed to stare at us out of pages. A few unfinished canvasses against the wall gave the whole place a kind of magic with their colors. They still held a faint smell of turpentine and paint, and you wanted to know about the artist who'd been there, what he was like. I tried to imagine. I asked the Kid what he thought, but he just shrugged.

Every once in a while, the Kid would stand around the staircase when Elena was there, as though trying to work up the nerve to ask if he could go back up. Like he wanted to breathe in whatever the painter had left behind. Whenever he was in the dining room, his eyes went roaming over those paintings. They grabbed me, too, like you'd entered a different world, with strange beings peering out from around trees and rocks in a fantastic landscape. One had angels in it—I guess they were angels, but no angels like I'd ever seen. They put me in a mood I had no words for, and I wondered how he knew to paint them.

And then there was Donovan.

"Well, Donovan, where have you been off to?" I asked him one day. I'd seen him dodge in and out but never there for long. He just gave me a big grin. Turned out he was having the time of his life. He'd been presenting himself as a celebrity. I heard him giving his spiel a couple of times at the bar—and with his charm and swagger he had three of the local lovelies falling at his feet. They cooked for him and lavished their attentions on him, like he was some kind of idol—and he made the most of it: a blonde one day, a redhead the next, a dark-haired beauty after her. Somehow he was getting away with it.

"What a place," he said to me once, walking out into the sunshine. "Perfect weather—it's the nuts." And he'd grin like he'd discovered all the secret of eternal happiness.

Curran pretended to ignore him, but he seemed to be keeping an eye out—absorbed in some project of his own. He kept popping up when you least expected, always with a notebook he scribbled in furiously. I caught a glimpse of little sketches. Once I asked him what had him so busy taking notes. "It's about human nature," he said. "A kind of philosophical biology both ontological and typological, but gathering up to the here and now—"

He looked pleased I'd asked, but I had no idea what he was talking about. "In a way," he said slowly. "I'm trying to dig out what's going to happen in the next moment by knowing the human type in action." He wouldn't say what sort of type, so I figured that was his way of putting me off—or on, without giving anything away. I wondered if he was just spying.

A couple of days later I saw his notebook lying on a chair in the bar, where he must have forgotten it. I had to see what he was up to. I took a look. Everybody was peculiar, he decided. They fell into certain types, by which they revealed their peculiarities: bird types, animal types, fish types. He thought he might be a mole type himself—he wasn't sure. Then I saw *GRACE—SNAKE TYPE. She moves with her body like she doesn't need legs. Curving in and under. Wouldn't trust her—wouldn't let her move too close. She could take you in her coils.*

Oh, dear, I thought, but I did have to laugh. He wasn't in any danger.

I noticed he spent a lot of time in the bar with a strange-looking tow-headed fellow, who had the face of an old child, the two of them always deep in conversation. The fellow was called Buck but he spelled his name Quambu'queau, which meant *This be Buck,* out of respect for him as an individual.

He had left his job in a ballpoint-pen factory in order, he said, to live without cramming his life full of mere things, and to invent a new language for a new age. One of his favorite words was *freeliness,* which meant not only a sense of freedom but freedom with generosity. An open hand.

He'd given away his belongings and now lived in a small shed over by the Hill of Holies. He'd collected some odd bits of furniture that others had thrown away and lived on fruits and vegetables from the grocery and bread from the bakery that could no longer be sold. He looked healthy enough, and always when I saw him he was cheerful and greeted me heartily. He seemed to enjoy watching people in the bar exchanging greetings and stories. Everybody knew him. Curran did lots of scribbling in his notebook. They made quite a pair. Peculiar enough for anybody.

And Billy—always with his finger on the pulse of things without ever letting on, so that he seemed to be guiding them with an unseen hand. He and the Kid still went out and around together.

So we slipped in and out of each other's presence, saying a few words here and there. We were like different species with different hours and pursuits—Curran wasn't all that far off.

I went about in my own way. The first time I saw her I was drawn to Rina and her garden. I was shy at first about approaching her, but after I told her how much I admired what she was doing and could I help her, she looked at me, smiled radiantly, and said, "Before we're done, you'll know everything I have to teach."

Every morning right after breakfast, we were out there together, working. At first I mostly watched, and she'd ask me to hand her this or hold that, telling me as she went along the names of plants and their families, pointing out the shapes of their leaves, the various uses of root, leaf, and flower. Maybe she was glad to have an apprentice. We spent hours with the sun on our backs, digging, weeding, watering, while she introduced me to her plants.

"And here is lovely Chamisa with her yellow flowers. Such a color for dyeing. She's pure gold. But even more—Old Mrs. Harter couldn't do without her—for her arthritis. Puts it in her bath. Lots of others too.

I started seeing plants and flowers as medicine, something in addition to what you saw or ate. That excited me. It felt good to have my hands in the dirt, to be planting things, helping them grow. I was being given a blessing—I was being released in ways I couldn't describe from the terrible state I'd been in. I kept looking at the life around me—it held discoveries. I woke up in the morning excited as a kid to see what the day would bring. Something different all the time, as we collected the flowers or leaves or dug up the roots of plants and tied them in bundles to dry. I got to know each new plant and what it offered. A new language. I had my own notebook and jotted down notes about their care, their uses as food, dye, and medicine.

"You know what this is?" Rina said one morning, pointing to a tall plant with yellow flowers.

"Mullein," I said proudly. That one I knew. It grew all over the yard back home. "Just a weed, isn't it?"

"Listen to the child," she said, putting her hand to her forehead. "Why it lets you breathe easy. Think of that. Softens the breath, takes away the coughing—bronchitis, asthma—they're a nasty business. The precious breath—what you can't live without. Just a weed indeed."

I should have known better.

"And this one, my dear Artemesia," she said. "Oh, what a gift! If you want to sleep and dream dreams, just sip her tea." I wondered if

I still had the power to dream. To dream past all I'd been caught in. Dreaming—it was what Dusty had done, it occurred to me, and what had it done for him? Turned him blind. Yet I couldn't help dreaming.

I hung onto Rina greedily, absorbed in the garden, not really paying attention to what was going on around me. Things were happening all right. Little volcanoes popping off. First Donovan got into trouble. A little explosion in the middle of the afternoon. Such a beautiful day, too. And here came the blonde with the wonderful chocolate cake Donovan loved. But pretty soon, the redhead appeared with her offering of a coconut cream confection—and just after that, the brunette with a lemon meringue pie. It was a great discovery, first the women ready to pull each other's hair out, then the realization that they'd been had. A great free-for-all, the women hurling their pastries, pelting Donovan with pie and cake and a lot of of bad language. Donovan's arms flailing, his tongue in motion as he tried to get a lick or two at the goodies hitting his face. Quite a show. Afterwards he got the ribbing he deserved. Then he swaggered around like nothing had happened. "I'm a big guy," he explained. "And my appetites . . . takes a lot to satisfy them." A pause. "Great fun while it lasted."

"Bullshit," I read over Curran's shoulder as he recorded an observation. Then he revised it. "Cock—and bull shit."

As the days grew into weeks I sensed a restless edge to Alta's doings. We hadn't spent a lot of time talking. "You okay?" I asked her.

"Oh, I'm happy enough—what's there to complain about? It's Dusty that's got me going. He's digging himself deeper into a hole—more like the grave. Doesn't care about anything anymore. Just getting drunk. Oh, men!" she said, throwing up her hands. "When aren't they a grief? What do you do with them?"

Suddenly, I knew we were all a little off balance. Restless. We'd never really come together to do our stuff. Nothing held us anymore, not really since Ventura City—we were just a bunch of oddballs thrown together. I loved hanging out in the garden, being with Rina, playing with the local kids when I wandered the streets. And yet there was something missing, something inside that wouldn't let me alone. I had no idea where I was headed, nor did anybody else, for that matter.

In the town everything seemed to be turning upside down. It was like their dream, what the townsfolk had come there for, was beginning to slip away right under their noses. They knew a threat was in the air, but they didn't know what to do.

No one thought much about it when Ronnie Earl Hoskins settled in New Town, across the river—just one more of the folks that had found their way to this out-of-the-way spot. Old Town had been a settled community for generations. But those in New Town were all looking for a fresh start and were in a tangle over what it ought to be. Lots of arguments and even a few fistfights. In an odd way Billy was the first to catch an inkling that something might be afoot. He amused himself in a variety of ways, and one of these was to read the want ads in the Weekly Trader. Often he read the ads aloud.

"Here's one," he'd say. "My fish outgrew my 30 gal. tank. Tin foil barbs, gold gourmals & plecos $25." Curran wanted to know if these were fish or parts of the tank.

"I've maybe heard of these," Billy said, all excited. "I'll bet they're like what I saw in the fishpond. I wonder where the fellow got them. It was like you could see through them."

Curran shook his head. "Maybe you can make them appear and disappear."

"Now there's an idea." Billy went on with the ads. "How about this: "Evangelist looking for a tent: 30' x 50' or larger. Also folding chairs."

"Just so I don't have to be in it," Alta said. "It's likely somebody's got something in mind that I'll want to step out of the way of."

I guess they did. For the Reverend, as Hoskins was called, had hit the ground running. His great vision, as he put it (for the voice in his head had set him on the track), was to build a great city in the desert. A holy city. And the immediate task for him was to build a wall, all the way from the river, taking in a big chunk of territory on the way, before it circled back to the river. He and his followers had hardly put up their makeshift shelters before everybody was put to work. All those who kept arriving were recruited for making bricks and adding on to the wall separating the two towns. It wasn't clear who was being shut out and who was to be inside and for what reasons. The wall was the thing, and it had the Old Towners worried. For rumors were in the air that Hoskins was claiming the land on our side of the river as well. And who did the land actually belong to? No one seemed to know.

I first saw Reverend Hoskins when he came around to the hotel, glad-handing all around, calling everybody Brother and Sister. A tall rangy fellow with a big-boned horsy face, splotchy red. I didn't like the way he laughed, his lips pulling up above his teeth like a dog getting ready to snarl and go for the jugular. He was ready to be excited that we were circus/carnival, whatever you wanted to call us. We could attract a public. Did we have a tent? When he found out I danced with snakes, he gave me a crooked look like a big question mark and wanted to know if I'd ever been bit.

"No," I told him. "Mine don't bite. And I keep my snakes well fed and take care of them. They won't harm anybody if they're treated right."

"You just do it for the money?" he said grimly.

"It's my living," I told him, looking him straight in the eye. *There were worse ways*, I could have told him.

"The first thing to living," he said, accenting the words, "is living right. You gotta tighten your loose living—that's my motto, given this world of sin and iniquity."

I didn't disagree. Only I wasn't sure what he had in mind.

"Believe me, Sister, I know—I've seen it all. Just hauling my semi back and forth—full of rabbit feed and chickens and pigs and you-name-it—across that blighted country from Carolina to California, Delaware to Dakota. But all my traveling has led me here . . ." Big grin. "For the big dream."

I didn't doubt it.

"You and me should set ourselves down and have a little talk sometime," he said.

That would be right chummy, I thought. There was a look in his eye that made me think of the way other men had looked at me, and if what was in his look wasn't on his mind, it had quarters in a murkier region.

"He's all primed with your good in mind," Alta said after he'd gone. And for reasons I couldn't explain, I felt like I ought to turn and run.

He had a message all right, and every Sunday he was out there in the square in front of the hotel to get it off his chest. For he'd had a vision, he told the crowd, and it was all about them, to shield all those who came there from the tide of evil that was engulfing the world. "Like most people," he said, "I started out with great hopes and big dreams for all of us to build the City of God on this earth. But that's not in the plan. Adam and Eve lost the chance for us there in Paradise. They had it and lost it for all of us and left us staring at a big dung heap."

He went on to paint the blackest of pictures. Lust and lechery and all kinds of perversions. Greed and violence and luxury. Books and films that glorified sin. Sodom and Gomorrah were only the beginning.

"We're far gone, Brothers and Sisters, polluting our bodies and the minds and hearts of the young. Oh, the demons that live in our hearts and minds! No wonder the wrath is coming to mow down vast numbers. No wonder the lost will lie, wailing and with the gnashing of teeth, writhing in their last agony."

But his city would be there for the few who turned their hearts in the right direction. That was the dream now.

At first some people snickered at him as he stood there in his cowboy hat and fancy shirt and silver-studded chaps and tooled leather boots, full of passion and dire warnings. Alexos just shook his head and in a low voice said, "There have always been sayers of doom, but we'd better be on the watch with this one. I'm afraid there's mischief brewing."

Before you knew it the air was full of rumors. It became clearer every day that the town itself was threatened. Hoskins was making a big push, claiming that no one had title to the land Old Town was built on. He was aiming to buy it up—cheap, no doubt, making the claim himself in the name of the great truckstop he was aiming to build, where folks could drive in any time and fill up with spirit.

Suddenly people were coming to meetings with the mayor in his office and to parlays at the hotel. Little clusters gathering and talking—a lot of protest and anger. People started making signs that said "Freedom for all," "Down with Tyranny," and "Leave us in peace,"

Even Billy and the Kid got into the act. Lettering up a storm. Early in his career Billy was a sign painter before he became an electrician and a magician, and he set himself up on the edge of the square with Bristol board and brushes. In deep concentration the Kid was wielding a brush. I thought about all the painting he'd done on the figures he had made, and how interested he was in the artist who'd lived in the hotel. The two were in their element.

As for myself, I was wandering around in a daze. Though I tried to keep up with Rina and the garden, she knew my heart wasn't in it. I couldn't help feeling all distracted, afraid something dark was going to break apart. And our place of rescue and all the dreaming that had brought people here would be trampled by somebody with a different dream that would push them out and shut the gate. For now it appeared that, unless the town could come up with a legal document that declared the town's right to exist, the Reverend was going to take it over.

A curious thing happened then at the hotel that had the family all in a dither. Alexos, that patient man who could repair anything, and who spent his days occupied with all the work of the hotel, who was devoted to his family and friends, who loved good food and conversation and spent his evenings engaged with others over his cigar and glass of brandy, suddenly withdrew and all but disappeared. Left off his work, his ladder standing near an outside window where he'd last used it; snatched a quick bite from whatever leftovers were around; and disappeared up into the attic. There he spent so many hours he was groggy when he came down.

Elena threw up her hands. "What possesses him—up there in all that dust?"

Nor could she tempt him to one of her delicious meals—his favorite dishes of lamb cooked in honey and lemon chicken and artichokes and good red wine. She was sure he had gone out of his mind. He was looking for something, he said, and please, she must not disturb him. This went on till Elena was almost distraught.

Then one evening Alexos emerged, dusty and weary but triumphant, waving a batch of papers.

"Come, dear," he said to Elena, taking her arm and summoning Leftheris.

"I've found what I was looking for," he announced as he entered the bar. "The town is safe." For a moment there was a hush as everybody quit talking and turned in his direction. "Right here—in my hand. The original charter granting the town the tract from the river to the Hill of Holies on to the hot springs and Coyote Canyon, signed by the governor of the Seven Cities Territory himself."

You never heard such a stomping and a cheering, folks crying out, "Speech, speech!" It was a great moment. Everybody knew it. And Alexos rose to the occasion, speaking of the great tradition that went back to the ancient Greeks. And how the town had been born from the great vision of his forebears, who proclaimed what it was to be human and what it meant to build a community where men and women could come and live in peace and freedom. It stirred my blood to hear his words and when he quoted from Pericles and Herodotus, men I'd never heard of but wished I had, I just wanted to cry. We all danced for joy.

Nobody got any sleep that night. The word spread like wildfire. Those who hadn't been on hand when Alexos emerged to make his great proclamation got the news in the next minute, and people came crowding into the bar to hear the story over and over and celebrate in style. Free drinks all around.

One of the young mothers held up her baby above the heads of the crowd, telling her to remember this moment because it was history and would be celebrated ever after in song and story. Even Captain Valor, who'd been at his mescal, managed to unglue himself from the bar stool and stagger up to offer Alexos his congratulations. He had to be discouraged from launching into the naughty version of "Sweet Betsy from Pike."

We didn't know how any of this would sit with the Reverend Hoskins, who'd been making such great progress with the wall you could hardly see the mountains from our side. He was going to ruin the view, Elena said. Alexos hoped that with the proof in hand, the other faction would rest content and go their separate ways on the land they occupied. Then the wall could come down.

Just at that moment Alta got a brilliant idea. Why not put on a big celebration for the town? Something that would demand the best from all the crew, and those others who wanted to take part. Something to be remembered for years. Carnival for the Gods—why not?

"That's what we're here for—right?" And it was time, she said, for us to get us off our duffs. Dusty was the one mainly on her mind. "If I can't get him moving, he's done for," she confided to me. "And I've got to do something about that big lug chasing all the skirts in town, and Eddie, who's gone completely peculiar. What a confounded lot," she said. "Your snakes fit for dancing?"

I'd gotten rather out of practice. Danced with them only once, one time in the bar. I took care of them, of course—they were my charge. I saw to it they got their mice and rabbits. I took them out and let them crawl around. I'd put them around my shoulders now and then. But I'd been neglecting them. I thought the celebration was a great idea, and so did all but Dusty.

"How are we going to get anything together?" he argued. "We've lost . . ."

"That's all over and done with," Alta said. "There's nothing like an opportunity waiting for you to take hold of. Whatever happened in the past, forget it."

"Come on," Dusty said. "We don't even have an elephant. Sam's gone, and the tiger with him. Quit giving me a hard time."

"You going to spend the rest of your life in that bar, corroding your liver and telling dirty jokes? Where's the old moxy?"

"Alta!" It was a wail.

But she wouldn't let up on him. She threw herself at him with all her passion and all the persuasion that was in her, till she wore him down, caved him in. Then, like magic, there was a real turnaround. The juice started flowing again, the old piss and vinegar, and he was hustling around, organizing, planning the acts, getting folks to contribute what was needed for props and costumes. There were conversations with the mayor and Alexos and other interested parties. It was to be held in the great ballroom.

Alta and I and a couple of the other women, Carol and Heather, looked through the costumes, saw what needed washing and mending and launched into the job. Plus we needed other outfits for the new performers. Several of the older women were delighted to help out, going through hats and dresses and finery, pulling things out of trunks, ready to sit for hours sewing and gossiping. They came up with a wonderful costume for Quambu'queau. Pantaloons and top of blue and orange, and a great mask with potato ears and a droopy mouth. He was to be the clown. He was thrilled.

And I was thrilled to be onstage again with my snakes. I'd danced with them that one time in the bar—the Kid and I did an act together. He'd made up a song about the loves of Pajarito, who'd turned from snake into bird and at some point into a man. Though the Kid still wasn't talking much, you could sometimes hear him singing. And he was at his old inventions. They lived in him. The stories we'd told together kept weaving through his mind, and then he'd pop up with a new creation. I'd catch him humming to himself at times and realized he was making up songs in his head. He had a good voice, clear and sweet, with a nice little huskiness at the edge. He was some kid all right. I figured maybe he and I could do another round for the celebration. He probably had another idea hatching. I was practicing with those snakes every day now, letting them get used to me and the moves again.

Things were coming along great guns. We were right in the midst of our preparations when, one morning, I went down to the basement to take the pythons from the heated cage where they were kept, and they weren't there. I couldn't believe it. The window had been jimmied, the wires cut, and the snakes were gone.

But who would have done it and why?

I ran up to Alta. "Somebody's stolen the snakes."

"Are you sure? That's crazy."

Who and why? Somebody fascinated with snakes? Not likely. Somebody who had a grudge and wished us harm—was that it? And if the snakes were set loose, where would they go? I tried scouting around. No luck. I was worried about them having been out at night in the cold. After a couple of hours I found them under a tree. They were hardly moving, and I knew they'd caught cold. I took them back, but later I could tell they'd already gotten pneumonia and there was no saving them. I burst into tears.

I was carrying them up to a vacant lot behind the hotel to bury them, when a little group of women came along with the Reverend Hoskins in their midst. He paused and indicated the others should go on ahead.

"Well," he said, "doesn't look like those snakes are much good to you anymore."

"They were beautiful," I said.

"Yes, all God's creatures are beautiful if they're put to the right use."

"And who are you to say?'

"I've seen the light," he said.

"And you . . . " I said harshly.

"I wouldn't touch your precious snakes. I got better fish to fry. And there's folks around who hate the whole idea of what you're doing—you and the others. Some pretty unhappy women."

I could hardly speak, I was so furious. "Who'd break in and steal just to kill harmless snakes and ruin everybody's fun?"

"Fun? Why look at you," he challenged me, "dancing with them in a bar. Profaning them and sinking yourself into the depths. That's your *fun*." He spit the word at me.

I turned on my heel to get away from him, but he grabbed me by the arm. "Now you listen here." I struggled to shake myself free and tried to kick him in the shin, but he pushed me against a tree.

"Listen here," he said. "You're standing on the edge—and you're looking down into the abyss. Yes, men and women take up snakes, as it's written. Mark 16, in the Holy Bible, not that you ever looked. But they do it for holy service—snakes with poison in them, and they dance for the sake of glory. If they're bit they're not harmed.

"That's not the way I heard it. Some have missing fingers—some die and leave their kids orphans."

He waved me off. "They dance for the glory. Not profaning what's holy, but taking up serpents to get beyond fear, for nothing then can harm them. Not the likes of you—all tinsel and hell spit, dancing for lust. You want to dance, there's snakes enough, real snakes with poison in them. One of my people has them. They're the snake hardly anybody sees, but he found 'em because he's the one chosen."

"I need a pair of snakes." I was mad enough to spit nails. I snapped out of his hold and pushed him aside.

"You want to tangle with them, do you? Go to the edge? Well, well. You think you can profane them? You think you can get away with it. We'll see."

He didn't bring them over himself. He cornered the Kid, who brought them in a box, a pair of snakes I'd never seen the likes of before, coppery color with black markings. Beautiful all right, but no doubt deadly, too. On top of the box was written, "Pichu cuate, a rare and special snake. A test of Grace."

I could see what that meant. There was venom in them all right.

I'd had a lot of experience with snakes. They were a part of me now, and there was a kinship between us. So that when I was up there dancing with them, the snakes and I, made one by our movements, were giving me a kind of knowledge. I was in touch with them by way of what went deeper than words, something that, though it came through me, came from beyond me. Lust, no. It was an energy I tapped into. It belonged to the body—that's where it started. But it didn't stop there. Because it filled me with joy as well, from the knowing. What did a man who'd got his reverend papers from the mail-order know about that?

I thought about what I should do. So long as I could control them, the snakes wouldn't be a danger to anybody. And I suppose something in me wanted to stand up to the Reverend's challenge. Others took up poisonous snakes and lived. So I'd keep them decently fed, but not so they were sluggish, and let them emerge from a basket and gently lift them onto my arm and around my neck. I knew how to hold them. First I had to get a sense of their temperaments, so I practiced in the basement. I'd pick them up gently and lead them around my arms and waist. They didn't seem to get upset.

Then I asked Billy and the Kid to watch me dance, and Dusty as well.

"Good show," they said.

I didn't tell them how I'd gotten them. "Somebody gave them to the Kid," was all I said.

Our efforts were gathering momentum. All sorts of people had stepped up to be in the show or help out with the production. A juggler named Boris, who'd once performed for the Dutch queen, came on board, and another pro, a bearded young guy, came around on his unicycle. There were musicians and dancers. Dusty was ecstatic.

"They're just showing up on their own," he said with amazement, "and I didn't have to do a thing."

We were well into rehearsals, and he was busier than three people put together, trying to get the timing right and the right sequence for the acts. He had us rehearsing for hours. He wasn't an impresario for nothing.

The great day arrived. All was ready. Flags of different colors flying in front of the hotel. Booths on the square and in the park, where folks could wander before and after the show. Candied apples and popcorn, fried dough and cotton candy. Beer and lemonade and soft drinks. Targets to shoot at, pins and beer bottles to tip over, a ring toss, games for the kids. Musicians playing. Afterwards, when everything was cleared away, the ballroom would be set up for dancing.

We were excited and full of glee. That afternoon we gathered to put on our costumes and makeup. Carol from the beauty salon was in charge of makeup, telling people to hold up their heads and not to smear their lips.

"Where's Buck?" Dusty asked. Nobody had seen him. "He should be out there working up the crowd." We looked around. We couldn't understand what had happened to him. He'd been all eager to be in the show. He thought the costume was out of sight, and he'd put in his time coming up with various antics. No Buck. We'd have to go on without him.

Just as we were about to begin the shivaree, letting everybody parade around the crowded ballroom—so many tickets had been handed out, we were going to have to do at least three shows—Buck appeared. He looked dazed, hardly able to walk, a large bruise on the side of his head. We crowded around him. He remembered that something whacked him, whacked him hard on the head just after he'd left his shed and then everything went black. When he'd staggered back to his shed, it was a pile of smoking cinders with a dented cooking pot in the middle.

We were caught up short. We'd gone on thinking that the two towns might put aside their differences and come together for the sake of the common good. We tried not to let the incident put a damper on the show we'd put together with so much labor and enthusiasm, and which was just ready to unfold.

Fortunately, Buck seemed to revive—there was no great injury, and we tried to help him get back into the spirit of things. He was still shaky, but once he got into his costume and had a good drink of water, he thought he could do it.

"The show has to go with Quambu'queau in it," he said, spelling out his name with his index finger.

There had been a delay. It was coming on sundown before everything was in place. We were behind the curtain and could see a few stragglers coming in, some from New Town as well. Alexos came backstage and said a little prayer over us for luck, for the renewal of our town. And then it all unfolded. I was the very last, and I was ready, one snake draped around my arm, the other around my neck. Suddenly, I caught the smell of something burning.

"Do you smell smoke?" I asked Billy, who'd just come backstage from his magic show.

He took in a breath. "I'm not sure," he said.

Dusty had just finished giving me a big fanfare, and I stepped out onstage to enthusiastic applause.

The smell was stronger. Then somebody yelled, "Fire!"

People began to panic, yelling and screaming, the performers leaping into the audience. I just stood there dazed, trying to stay calm for the sake of the snakes. before I could move, Billy leapt onto the stage.

"Come on, Grace, " he yelled, trying to grab me, "we've got to get out of here."

"Get away," I yelled. "What are you doing?"

For the snakes his frantic gesture was a threat. And the next thing I knew one of them had struck him on the hand.

XIII.

Billy was gone—oh, how could it have happened?—and his magic had leaked away—out of the world and into the dust. His absence was a hole the wind roared through, a socket where an eye had been, a howling dark wind, and we were undone. It was clear now how much he'd held us together, cleared the way out of the zigzagging confusion we were so often snarled in. The one who helped Alta see straight when she sent the air crackling. The one who kept his distance when Curran and Donovan went at it tooth and nail and, at just the right moment, entered the fray to kid them back to sanity. And the Kid . . . Knowing how everybody felt. Never laying blame when he could have. He rescued Dusty and me, kept rescuing us all. Only now there was no rescue and only a horrible voice in my ear.

You thought you had it all figured out, didn't you? quivering those hips and giving the dudes a hard-on. There's hell, there's damnation.

Lost now. The Kid maybe more lost than anybody. Oh, the magic there. Took that bundle of chaos and worked it into something halfway human. Showed him there was a way to live in the world without beating on yourself or somebody else. How to have pleasure in what the day offered . The magic of being alive. The Kid took it all in like sunlight and air. Before Billy, he had only what I could give him. Billy held him spellbound—the one person he listened to, tried to live up to.

The Kid wanted to be a magician, with all the tricks. Wanted to take Billy's sleight of hand and add a few more flourishes. Father and mentor, that's what Billy became, the one who showed him his path. All for the sake of magic. When Billy was gone, the Kid sat there numb, huddled in the cape Billy gave him during that terrible hour at the end. His legacy. Told the Kid he had to carry on.

For days on end, the Kid just sat there, torn from the world Billy had given him, Billy's blue velvet silk-lined cape around him, playing solitaire for hours, never saying a word. His silence seemed more dangerous than ever. Refused to eat. When the numbness gave over and the rage boiled up, there was no living with him.

Alta was caught in the agony of helplessness, having to watch Billy slip away and deal with the aftermath. Too late when we got him there to that outpost of the future. Too late to save him in that shining city that was not only up to the minute with everything imaginable, but had shot way past it. Everything sleek with invention, the latest technology. You should have seen the hospital—half run by robots, smarter than most people you know. Could even do surgery, all with light beams. The computers were a marvel, the doctors all on screens talking to you like they were practically sitting in your lap, ready to answer your questions. And over it all was a little group of humans who did nothing but spout ideas and do math and graphs and paperwork. There in a little tower above the shining corridors where you could come to shed your pain and troubles and rise up whole and new. All designed with perfection in mind.

And the city too, ATLANTIA—no small letters for a city so big and bold and brilliant—with its broad avenues and palm trees and domes and columns—a marvel. Beautiful beyond anything I'd ever beheld. But without Billy what did it matter? We pleaded with him not to leave us.

"We need your magic," we wept.

"There'll be more," he promised, and sank into a dream beyond us. How could we believe him?

Even now I can't say it all straight. Things come—bits and pieces out of that time, in a harsh glaring light. My head was reeling then with what had happened, and I couldn't see past my hand.

You killed him, all right. It's the pride that goeth before a fall . . . Poison in your hands, unholy hands. The hands of a harlot in this cesspool of a world. Fall to your knees . . .

Even in my sleep I could hear the hiss of that voice. What I'd travel with till the end of my days. Oh, Billy, I never meant any harm.

Alta refused to go back to Old Town. Not in a million years would she set foot in that cursed place. Nor I. Dusty and the others had to collect our trailers. With some help, they brought over the caravans. And finally, we ended up leaving them, too.

Alta was in a sweat to be on the road again. ATLANTIA? She couldn't stay there either. Didn't belong there any more than a stray cat. Nor did the rest of us.

"I'd just be kept a prisoner of memories," she said, opening her palms. We stared at her blankly. "So what do you want me to do?" she said angrily. "I've got to get out of here, keep moving till I fall in my tracks. Stay here all of you. Just let me go on my way."

Abandon us? And what would happen to her? To us?

"But the Carnival?" Donovan protested.

"Are you nuts? What Carnival?"

I wanted to comfort her, but what could I say? It'll all work out. We'll find our way. Straws in the wind. Cactus thorns.

"And you," she said to me, "you better be looking out, making tracks." She took an envelope from her pocket, all creased and crinkled, and pulled out a letter, "It's the second one the damned fool has had the gall to send."

"Priam?" I couldn't believe I was saying his name.

"The one and only. Some people will keep coming at you no matter if you kick them where it hurts, which I intend to do if I ever lay eyes on him."

"What does he want?"

"Just guess."

I didn't have to. He was coming to get me, all right, so he could make some more money off me. Even now, he was on his way to the Seven Cities Territory to lasso me and bring me back.

"I'm eighteen," I said, as if somehow that was my protection. "Just let him try."

And suddenly, she had her arms around me.

"Okay," she said. "We'll stick together. That's all we can do now. Anybody got a better plan?"

Nobody did.

I can't even say how it happened, how we quit wandering about in a daze. How we came to know about the fiesta. All I know is that one day we took flight over the mountains, on the way to somewhere else. I'd never been in a plane before, and my stomach kept trying to head up to my throat. I couldn't look below—it made me dizzy, so all I could do was hope we'd land before my stomach did. There were great peaks to look at, great canyons to sink your eyes into, all turned golden by the sun, but I had to keep my eyes away from the window. We were on top of the clouds, and my head was spinning out into the stratosphere. Donovan was having a hard time for different reasons, cramped in that little space. When we landed, it took two big guys to hoist him out. Alta was deep in some dream of her own, and Dusty sat stock still beside her, hardly blinking. The Kid hunkered inside his cape, deadly quiet, not looking out. Curran slept, wheezing a little. He had it best of all.

"Just want you to know I don't give a rat turd about this festival, whatever it is," Alta said before we landed. "It's just an excuse to keep moving, that's all. Nothing to lose. Something to fill in the time."

Curran, awake as we bounced into the landing, kept biting his nails. Raw nerves all around me. Still hollow. We were at least on the ground.

When we got off the plane and were taken by the waiting buses down to the river, we were pulled into the press of people, a crushing throng. Couldn't help being scared and shaky. So much din and confusion all at once. People must have come from everywhere, whole families with kids big and little, bringing their tents and bundles and baskets of food. But then in front of the big tent set up for the arrivals, hosts and hostesses met us all and led us towards the boats waiting to go up river.

We were surrounded by signs of welcome, and offered water, which we drank thirstily, and mangoes, slices of papaya, and passion fruit. When we got to the river the landing, too, was overflowing with people. Musicians lugging their instruments, clowns and actors, storytellers, and vendors, all who'd come for festivities. A colorful bunch, ready for a good time.

"Stay close," Alta said, looking around anxiously. We stood and waited in our little huddle. A black dog without its owner came up to nuzzle my hand, eager to be petted. She had pups somewhere, for her teats were full. She licked my hand and kept looking up at me, stayed close and wouldn't leave my side for a time. Seemed like she knew I needed her. I hoped she would stay, but the smell of food was in the air, lots of scents to sniff after. We watched as people boarded the ferries and barges at the docks. As soon as one boat filled, another pulled up for the next group.

"Good grief," Dusty said, as he surveyed the scene, and let it go at that.

I couldn't hear myself think in all that din. Musicians playing, kids yelling, pulling at their mothers' arms, demanding to know how soon they'd be there, babies crying, dogs barking, vendors crying their wares above the noise, boatmen cursing as they tried to keep people from shoving for a place on the boat.

"You'll all get there, friends," one of them yelled. "There's time for everything. You don't have to worry about time here."

I was so afraid we'd be separated or trampled, I clung to Donovan since he was a head above the crowd. Curran must have had the same fears, and Donovan stood there laughing down at him, trying to gig him for sticking close. Curran was getting red in the face.

"Stop bullying," Alta commanded. "You're worse than any kid."

Suddenly the whole mood changed. People started passing around bottles of wine and beer. A couple of young guys, all grin and muscle, sent a stream into their mouths from a pot with a spout shaped to do that. Didn't miss a drop. The spectators cheered. Someone pulled out a bottle of mescal. We were all drinking with our new buddies, making jokes, breaking into laughter, caught up in good cheer in spite of ourselves. Only the Kid stood back.

Then food appeared. Little flaky pies filled with meat, tamales made with potatoes or filled with chicken. Little seed cakes. How good everything tasted!

"What is this place?" Alta asked a young woman bouncing a baby in her arms. She looked at Alta, astonished. "You don't know? Why, Mecharlinda. And you've never been to the festival? Ah, wait'll you see. There's no experience like it."

The excitement was contagious—what with the tastes of food and wine to satisfy hunger and thirst, enough even to satisfy Donovan. His face had the look of bliss. Then all there was to see: boats decorated with flowers and ribbons, all in brilliant colors, and the women in their embroidered blouses and skirts.

I tried to let go of everything, just like I did at my first circus, not sit there and huddle over my grief—I'd never wear that out. Everybody had entered the gaiety. More people kept pouring down, standing along the banks, waiting for boats. The music took us up—fiddles and guitars playing in spite of the noise. I tried to move a little closer to a trio of them, guitar, fiddle and clarinet, so I could hear, but still keeping an eye on the others, especially the Kid. I'd get all caught up in the spirit around me; then something would snag me, and I'd go spiraling down.

Oh, Billy—you should be here!

"Come, Paloma, don't look so near to tears," an old woman said as she stood beside me. She patted my arm. "You'll get a place on the boat." I tried to smile. She looked at me more closely. "You'll find all you need to ease your heart." She handed me a flower. Its scent was as sweet as belief, and after I held it to my nose, I kept hold of the little yellow flower carefully.

We did find a place on the next boat and the old woman, whose name was Evelina, said. "Here, move over this way so you can see. There are lovely things along the way."

The boat was in no hurry at all but moved along slowly into the current, the countryside unfolding before us. I turned my eyes into a day all balmy and sweet with a circus of clouds above us, the light sliding along the water in patches of brilliance. Blue and green, then a diamond dazzle. For the moment I was filled with air and light, not even taking notice any more of the folks around me. Then the breath went out of me. Not just at the sight of the hills with their forests and the river flooded with light, but the gardens going down to meet it.

Then Evelina said, "The City of Gardens—that's the meaning of Mecharlinda." Roses and bougainvillea—orange, lemon, guava, apricot, almond, and lime trees covered with fruit and flowers all at once—and jacarandas all in blue blossoms.

When I looked up at a figure that had appeared in front of me,

I saw a boy standing there, perhaps Evelina's grandson. He held up a garland of carnations and blue flowers I didn't recognize and bent over to place it around my neck.

"There," Evelina said. "Breathe in the scent, and all will be well. You are here in this precious moment—to enjoy the festival."

I wanted to. I wanted Alta and the others to enjoy it as well, in spite of all that had happened, in spite of the empty space of the future before us. When I looked at Alta, she seemed lost in wonder at something she had seen. Perhaps the gardens. Later she told us about a girl she had caught sight of, in a silvery costume riding a bay horse, light as a feather, and then another figure, a boy sitting on a rock, playing a flute.

I'd have been happy to continue in the slow movement of the river, just letting go of time and being carried along forever, but we'd come to a dock. A series of maneuvers jolted us, then the rattle of chains, and we were tied up at the pier, soon launched into a new kind of activity.

We were off the boat and into streets now, crowded with all those who'd arrived before us, making their way towards the center of town.

"We're just in time," Evelina said, coming up behind us as we tried to get our bearings. "The parade is like no other. Now it all begins," she said. "Have courage." She looked at me intently, pressed my hand, and disappeared into the crowd. I waved to her—glad she had been there.

We were making our way, following the crowd, managing to keep together. Donovan was steering us through the thronged street when a voice above us called down, "Hola, strangers. I can see you've come from who-knows-where and have never been here before."

We looked up to see a man bending over the railing of his balcony, the sun glancing off a mostly bald head, circled with long gray hair.

"Come up here to watch the parade. This is the perfect spot." Gratefully, we accepted the invitation, all but Donovan, who decided to take his chances down below. He could see over everybody.

"Bienvenido," Don José greeted us and introduced himself. "A great pleasure to see you here." A tall man, he was dressed for the festival in a black vest over a white ruffled shirt, with a belt of silver disks surrounding the waist of his black trousers—distinguished-looking with his white sideburns and mustache. He stood as though he'd been waiting just for us. "You'll be able to see the whole procession."

We arranged ourselves while he turned his attention to the Kid.

"You are here to see—wonders," he told the Kid, as though he was the one who could best appreciate them, "—the way these animals move. All the wild ones. No collars or muzzles or leashes. Think of that. They keep their wild hearts."

Wild hearts. For a moment I caught an image of Antoinette and Caruso, and the thought of them made me wish I could see them down there.

A flare of trumpets. Music. And a figure leapt out, dressed in motley. "The Prince of Folly," Don José said.

I watched him run towards the crowd brandishing his scepter, bells jangling. The Kid, all eyes, stood at Don José's side.

"Can't do without him," he said to the Kid. "Every once in a while you have to turn things inside out so they'll come up right. Otherwise—"

He let it go at that. The clown zigzagged back and forth, making faces, sticking out his tongue, making obscene gestures and remarks that sent the crowd into an uproar. Cuddling up to the women, producing a huge zucchini to impress them, challenging the men, reaching his arms towards the little kids, and twirling those around who would go to him.

The elephants followed, all decked out with tasseled blankets and headpieces, swinging their trunks, humping along in their slow swaying gait, legs like moving tree trunks, young boys and girls on their backs.

"Where did they get all those elephants?" Dusty wanted to know. "Astonishing." Our one little elephant was who knows where? For a moment Dusty had a look of chagrin, envy maybe.

The Kid was hanging so far over the railing, I was afraid he would land in the midst of the crowd below and be trampled to bits. Alta and I exchanged looks and decided he was okay. Don José nodded, gave us a little quirk of a smile. He was looking out for him.

A pause. The elephants separated into four groups, rose up and placed their forelegs on the backs of those in front, their trunks held high in the air.

"Holy—" Dusty stopped himself. "Look at that, will you?" he said, more to himself than to us. "At least a dozen. I never had more than four." The crowd cheered and whistled as the elephants rearranged themselves and moved on.

We continued clapping as the big cats followed: lions and tigers, jaguars and leopards, muscles rippling, all in their pride of their patterned, sleek bodies. All kinds of animals, gazelles and ibexes, dromedaries, camels, and llamas—the hoofed and horned—carried themselves between the cheering crowds, their eyes focused ahead. No chains on any of them, their trainers following quietly behind.

"Animals from all over the world," Don José told us. "I've watched this parade since I was a boy. Always a thrill. And it was all done nearly two thousand years ago. Think of that. The Romans came up with the idea, and some of their descendents found their way here. From that warlike race a peaceful parade of animals—think of that."

"I've never seen anything like it," Alta said. She couldn't fathom how they managed it all without the beasts tearing into the crowd.

"You have to keep them all well fed," Don José said. "It's hungry animals you have to watch out for—and fearful ones."

He was enjoying our wonder, I could tell. Then he waved his hand as though he, himself, was making it all appear. It was just the beginning . . .

For Dusty the parade must have brought a bitter edge to his admiration. He just kept shaking his head, as though put to shame by a spectacle he could never match. More and then more, the spectacle was building. Here came chariots and carriages, high stepping horses with Indian riders; clowns by the dozen on tricycles, unicycles, donkeys, and wagons. Others on foot, bouncing and tossing balls, turning somersaults, pulling wagons with dogs sitting in them, giving their doggy grins to the crowd. Then great paper maché figures like they'd emptied the books of heroes and giants, fairies and mermaids, figures from the zodiac. Color and music, and a day full of streamers and confetti.

"They spend the whole year preparing for this," Don José told us. "They've got it down to a gnat's eyebrow. Practicing all the time. Ah, when I was young and in my prime . . ."

Then, right at the center of the parade, were the acrobats, first the ones doing the leaps and somersaults from the backs of horses, then those leaping through rings of fire, their red costumes bright with suns and moons. Made me giddy to watch. Dusty was beginning to look blank—it was too much for him. The Kid's eyes bugged out.

Curran said, "Where are the midgets?"

Alta turned to me and I could see a sparkle of tears. "Oh," she said. "Oh my."

"What's the matter?" I asked her.

"Nothing. Nothing. I just can't bear to have it end."

Neither could I. It had all been so . . . how could I say? Beyond my imagination.

The parade was over, the spectacle done, and we were back in our skins, looking at one another like we'd come down from another planet. Below us in the streets, the crowd began to disperse, the spectators headed towards the other delights of the festival. We had no idea what all lay ahead of us. We thanked our host for having given us such a rare treat and descended into the melee. I'd seen Donovan in the midst of the throng watching eagerly, but when we were down in the thick of it, there was no sign of him. He'd just vanished.

"Now how does somebody that big manage to evaporate?" Dusty wanted to know.

And though we tried to keep together as we threaded our way through knots of people caught up in celebration, I got separated from the rest. For a time I couldn't move through the mass of people. After a struggle to get anywhere at all, I maneuvered to the edge of the crowd and ducked into one of the backstreets, where there were fewer people. I had no idea which way to go, except to try to find my way down to the river, back to the landing, so I could set out from there again. A confusing business in that maze of streets, with little corners and squares and alleys going off who knows where. Lots of little shops open for the celebration, displaying banners from their doorways—cakes and cookies and masks and costumes in their windows. I got all tangled up, my head completely turned around.

Alta had the only map of the town with the locations of the various festivities, but how in the world would I find her? It took forever to work my way through the streets, but then somehow I reached the edge of a place open and clear, and I was able to breathe. I had come to the entrance of a park, perhaps at the center of the city.

As I began walking along the path, I saw it was a huge park, planted with all kinds of trees and shrubs, from acacias to palm trees. Roses—pink, white, red, and yellow—sunned themselves, taking in the light. There were arbors of magenta and red bougainvillea and red and yellow cannas all around; bird of paradise and elephant ears, as well as great showy pink and white blooms I'd never seen before. Here and there along the paths and alongside a pond were benches where you could sit and watch the swans and ducks, now with their babies. Lovers were strolling about or lying on blankets spread out on the grass. Families, too, had set up house on the grass, with their tents and cooking pots, their kids playing on the slides and swings, their dogs romping around. The smell of food sent my juices flowing. I could smell spices and chili, rich and savory.

I longed to find one of the vendors. I was so hungry I could have eaten the roses, but I saw no food stands or vendors. A woman stirring a pot simmering on a grill looked up, spotted me, and beckoned me over. The smell coming from the pot made my stomach growl.

"Hello, stranger, welcome to the festival." she said.

I thanked her. I couldn't keep my eyes from what she was cooking.

"Are you hungry?" she said.

"The food smells wonderful."

"Come join us for our meal."

I didn't need a second invitation. She was a few years older than me, with a crown of black hair like crows' wings, and bluish lights, like Jessie's, and high cheekbones like hers. She wore several strands of turquoise and silver over an elaborately embroidered collar. And there were swirling designs in her long skirts. She was beautiful, I thought. As she stirred the food, she would glance over at a little girl, perhaps three or four, who sat at the edge of a blanket playing with her toes.

"You are alone?" she said.

"I have no idea where I am. I lost my friends."

"It is hard to find your way alone. The first time it's hard for strangers."

I was relieved I had found her.

"You've come at the right moment," she said. "I am Antonia and my girl is Elizabeta. Please sit down and rest. We'll eat as soon as the boys come back. They're with their father at the pond, swimming. They couldn't wait for the fiesta—they talk about it for weeks before and then for weeks after."

Antonia's two sons came running up, their towels around their shoulders, shivering a little, eagerly clamoring for their *almuerzo*.

"We're hungry as tigers," said their father, coming up behind them. Antonia started filling bowls with chicken mole, rich with chocolate, chili, and spices. She passed a bowl to each of us, then dipped one out for herself. A plate of tortillas went round. The boys snatched at them eagerly. But before we ate, she had the older boy, Jorge, say a little prayer of gratitude. Then gratefully, we began to eat. It was a joy to be in the open air and sun, dipping tortillas into the wonderful dish.

The park, too, had come alive with celebration, as various figures began to whirl past us, people in costume filling the park, pausing to comment on each other's fancy dress, showing themselves off, flirting from behind masks with elaborate gestures.

"Ah lovely one . . . you have stolen my heart. Meet with me at the Southern Gate."

"Ah, you rogue."

"I see such sparkle in your eyes . . . what is there behind that mask?"

"So, handsome one, do you want to see me without my mask? That might be too much for you . . ." Some couples spiraled off together.

Flutes, clarinets, kettle drums announced something special, and the figures stepped back, pausing to watch as four men came forward, each holding up a pole attached to a fancy-looking covered stretch-er—I guess you'd call it—carrying whoever was inside. A number of young women walked alongside, dressed in Turkish trousers and vests all embroidered and trimmed with gold. It looked like they were servants to the one lying inside, fanning him with peacock and ostrich feathers, feeding him grapes, figs, guavas, mangoes, bananas as fast as he could toss them down. Then a head popped out and a hand motioned to one of the ladies in a filmy bodice and pantaloons.

I could hear him, "Sweet one, my little honeybun, this throat is mighty damned parched and dry. Could we have a little potion of the blessed grape?"

That voice! . . . Could it be? I held my breath as she poured a goblet full from her carafe, and he downed it in one swallow, then held out the goblet for another round. As the figure sat up and leaned out, a sultan with turban and lavender shirt, I recognized the old snake-in-the-grass himself. Priam Gillespie!

I gasped. If he could be anything, it was a sultan with a bevy of beauties waiting on him hand and foot, pouring wine into him, and feeding him till he popped a gasket. I didn't know whether to laugh or turn and run. How had he managed to get here? Priam. Sultan.

It was too much. Quickly I turned away, hoping he wouldn't recognize me.

Antonia was looking back and forth from one to the other. "You look like you've seen a ghost," she said.

"A ghost, all right," I said, with a quick glance over my shoulder.

Still he leaned out, beckoning. Out of the corner of my eye I watched as the young men set down his conveyance and two of them helped the sultan descend, offering a steadying arm. He wavered back and forth for a moment, came to a second's balance, lost it, reached for an arm, took the carafe of wine from the young woman, and bungled his torso down the path. A couple of peacocks browsing in the neighborhood let out a shriek. Took him by surprise. He reeled, steadied himself against a tree.

Antonia's boys let out whoops of laughter, and the rest of us broke down as we watched. Priam, with the help of the tree he leaned against, primed himself with a few more swigs. Then he gathered himself together and stumbled along.

I thanked Antonia and her family for their hospitality and then started off myself, a little way behind Priam. I wanted to see where he was going and think what I ought to do. In his present condition there wasn't much harm in him; I could lose him easily in the crowd. But since he was after me, I didn't want to be taken by surprise and be caught unprepared.

He wandered into another part of the park, where men and woman were sitting on blankets spread out on the grass with their baskets of food, their clothes discarded around them, picnicking in the grass or wandering the paths hand in hand. Priam stopped dead in his tracks. All those beautiful women without a stitch on.

"They're all starkers!" he cried out, almost in a shriek, like lightning had struck him with the vision of a new prospect for himself. His head swiveled in every direction, gawking at a pair of gay lovers sitting under a tree; an older woman offering a kiss to a man no longer young, who was yearning towards her; a young man offering his companion a cup of wine. She took a sip and gave it back to him, holding him with her eyes. He drank deeply and sat for a moment gazing into hers. Then both rose; he put his arm around her waist, and they sauntered towards a grove of trees.

I saw Priam crouch behind a bush, and when he rose, his silken pantaloons and embroidered shirt were gone. He stood there, gut hanging out, naked as a pin-up, except for his turban and the carafe he carried. I put my hand over my mouth. He hobbled along on bare feet. A wonder he could walk at all, considering what he'd put down his gullet and into his gut. But when he could fill his eyes with women, he could move like greased lightning.

I followed him, keeping my distance, watching him leer and drink and scratch his belly, offering his carafe to the giggling women who ducked away into the trees, leaving him scratching his head in bewilderment. I could almost see the line of his lips, his face going mean.

And I ducked away too. He wasn't going to be part of my life. Not any longer. I knew at that moment my life was going to change, and I had to be the one to pick it up from whatever pieces it lay in and move on. I felt a catch in my chest for what I'd have to leave behind. I'd gone with the Carnival as far as I could go. It had given me a home. But that was over. I needed a place where I could have a life. No one was ever going to own me again.

I was hard put to it to find my own way. First I had to find Alta and tell her goodbye. Hard, hard for me to do, she meant so much to me. I knew, too, that I'd have to leave the Kid behind, and I had to be sure he'd get taken care of, handful that he was. Somehow I knew he would be okay. It would all be hard. Before I knew it, I was walking through the park crying for the Kid, because of what lay before him, and for Alta because she'd loved me, and that was her great gift. And for Billy, because I'd handed him his death. I'd even miss Donovan and Curran.

"Hey, lovely one, why those tears. It's a time for celebration."

I put on a smile for the man who was passing me.

"It makes me cry," I said. "It's all so beautiful."

It was harder than I knew when I found her on the other side of the park and felt her arms around me. Just seeing the sadness in her eyes, even though she was smiling, too. Maybe she already knew, could sense my leaving in her bones.

"It will be all right," she said, hugging me close. "All will be well."

She'd break it to the Kid at the right moment and tell the others. "You'll find your way, amazing girl. Don't let what's happened spoil your life. In the carnival anything can happen."

And then I was alone, more alone than I'd ever been. It was like I'd put on a cloak made out of all the blue moments I'd ever known. Just sinking back into them. I'd made a terrible mistake. She'd loved me, she'd pulled me through the terrible things that had happened. What was I supposed to do? I wasn't anybody any more. I sat down under a tree and tried to pull myself together. I leaned back and closed my eyes but opened them quickly. A darkness seemed to blur everything—the flowers and trees, the revelers in their costumes, the music in the distance.

You've not said goodbye to me—why you haven't even said hello. Disap-

pearing before you've ever appeared. That's not cricket. That's not being the trouper that you are.

"Billy!" I cried, leaping up from under the tree. I recognized the voice before I made anything out. There seemed to be a presence floating a little above the ground, not quite real and yet somehow more real than I could imagine.

"Oh, Billy," I blubbered. "It's because of me that . . . I killed you."

Nonsense. You see me here don't you? You think I'm a figment of your imagination? Maybe that doesn' even matter. After the hard *part, I tell you, I just unzipped my skin and stepped right out, easier than pie. Never did such a disappearing act before. What a stunt! And you know what that means?*

I had no words.

Why now you see me like I am. The real-io, tru-lio Billy. How easy to be part of the dream. And you there moping under that tree. You've not even got your costume. And you're supposed to be dancing here like all get-out.

"How could I? After what's happened? How could I even pick up a snake again?"

Why you've got to live up to your name. It's in the stars, though you got to be the one to choose. And you don't want to disappoint yourself. Surely not.

He was beginning to disappear while I was standing there feeling more naked than the figures there in the park.

I've just got to do something for Billy, to make things up to him, I thought, with a sinking heart. Only it seemed like he lifted the idea from my mind.

No, you've got it all wrong. It's not me you've got to do anything for—it's yourself. That's the hardest thing. And you're at the beginning. You don't even know what's in the package.

I couldn't make out his presence anymore

"Oh, Billy, don't go." I knew it was useless to ask, but I wanted so much to hold onto him, I could hardly hear what he was saying.

I've told what I have to tell, darling. And I'm going to join the fun. I've got to see you dance. And believe me I'll be on hand to watch. I'm your biggest fan.

I stood there for a long moment with the late afternoon sun dappling through the trees, trying to get hold of Billy's words. It seemed like an echo floated in the air. Amazing. Amazing. Amazing.

I was restless and nervous, could hardly stand still. I started off again with no idea where I was headed. A whole chapter of my life had closed, but where was the beginning of the next? I didn't even know where I'd spend the night. There was still a lot going on in the park, but my mind kept whirling in circles, Billy . . . Alta . . . the Kid . . . and all we meant to one another.

Just before I turned off the path I saw several small groups in costume cross the park. When one of them approached, a woman left the group and came towards me as if she wanted to speak to me. Her dress immediately caught my eye, a light and silvery web that glistened as it fell around her hips, changing colors, mostly blues and greens, as she moved. Around her neck she wore a chain of carnations, pink and white. When she stood in front of me, I could read a little card attached near her shoulder, Selena . . . Mistress of Mysteries.

"Hello, my dear, I see you're all alone," she said. "If you don't know your way around, perhaps I can help you."

"I'm alone now, and I think I'm lost. I'm trying to get back to the river."

"I see you don't have a costume. Do you know where to go?"

I wasn't sure what to say. "I don't know about costumes—I see people wearing them."

She smiled. "Oh, you'll have something new to experience. Will you come with me?"

She seemed to be inviting me for something I hesitated to do right then—just letting myself follow what was offered without knowing what I was getting into. I'd been betrayed once too often. And though it seemed harmless enough, just getting a costume, I wasn't ready to do it.

"It's part of the festival," she insisted gently. "A long tradition. Those who've come too late or for some other reason didn't get costumes feel they've really missed out—they admit it themselves."

I didn't know what to say.

"I see you're full of questions—I sense you're not ready. So I'll leave you. But if you change your mind, you can find me. Just ask for Selena." She pointed in the direction of a building that had brilliant tiles decorating the walls and an arched doorway. "That's where the costume rooms are and the helpers. I'll be there as soon as I get a bite to eat, and for a couple of hours before the crowning of the King of the Sun and the Queen of the Moon. It's a great moment," she said. "Whatever you do, don't miss that." She pointed me towards the river.

She'd halfway convinced me, and I didn't want her to leave me alone to fret. I'm not sure why I still dragged my feet, but something turned me back towards the river almost as if I was being pulled by a magnet. It wasn't easy to get there or anywhere—another wave of people filled the park and the streets beyond. I was going against the tide. Voices murmured around me.

I was in their path.

"You're on the inside of the wrong way."

"The fiesta's just beginning. Why'd you come, if you want to leave so soon?"

Fortunately, just ahead of me were several men in light blue uniforms directing people along various paths.

"Where are you going, Señorita?" one of them asked me. I told him I was trying to get to the river.

He pointed out the direction and told me not to take the broad avenue that led directly to the landing but to turn off on a side street. He held up his hand for people to pause and let me through.

I thought I understood his directions, but I missed the turn and found myself doing what he'd told me to avoid. I was immediately engulfed by the crowds in the broad avenue that led down to the landing. I caught a glimpse of the water in the late sun and paused to catch my breath. So now what? I needed to find a place to stay. With so many people in the town, I figured I'd need a real stroke of luck. I might have to sleep in the park. I was so absorbed trying to think what to do next I had no eyes for anything around me and made people move aside so I wouldn't bump into them.

"If you're not all tied up this evening . . ." The voice, somehow familiar, was directed towards me. "I could do with a little company for the fiesta."

Startled, I looked up into the man's face. I was seeing another ghost. Only this one looked real. "Ben! How in the world! Ben!" I threw my arms around him. "How did you get here? How did you find me?"

"Well, for starters, I was looking for you. Madly looking for weeks. And finally, I landed here. What a place! 'This is where you'll find her, if she's to be found.' That's what they told me. 'Perhaps a doorway will open. It's always possible. Chance lives here. Special encounters. Lovers are drawn together. Quarrels reconciled.' That's what they say, with a clap on the shoulder, a big grin. But this much is true." He hugged me again.

The crowd kept jostling us, threatening to separate us. He pulled me aside to the edge of one of the shops, and we just stood for a moment, taking each other in. He was there—he was actually there.

"But come," he said. "Let's see what this festival is all about. Are you hungry? I'm starved. Been wandering around all day."

He had hold of my hand, and I was trying to keep up, overwhelmed. I was weak in the knees. I kept my eyes on him, as though he might fade and disappear like Billy had done. But Ben was really there, leading me back in the direction of the park. Now we were in the flow of the crowd, the whole surging wave, the two of us in the midst of it. I tried to imagine how he'd got himself over the mountains into Ventura City, traveled the road to the ruins, found his way to Old Town. Had he heard of the terrible events—the Reverend, the fire, Billy, oh Billy—Then to ATLANTIA, asking around for news of us. Found his way to the fiesta. And come upon me in the midst of all this crush . . . I still couldn't believe it.

"Jessie told me about you," he said. "All your dreams about getting to Las Vegas and starting a new life. She was all upset and worried about what happened. She could hardly stand to be there after you were gone. Blamed herself for not keeping tabs on Priam. She's been talking about leaving ever since. When she heard the old goat say he was coming to get you, set you up as one of her girls, she told him it was all over."

"I've seen him—" I told him how Priam had been transformed into a sultan and was wandering around in his skin, chasing the girls.

"The old letch!" He's always known what his life was about, he said.

"You can say that much, I suppose."

Which was more than I did. At the moment, I hardly knew whether to laugh or cry.

"He won't get far here, I'll bet. Don't worry, he'll have me to tangle with at least."

"But you're supposed to—"

He stopped and gave me a look both tender and accusing. "You think I was just going to put you out of my mind and go bury my head in business courses and not give a damn what happened to you? I told my professors there was an emergency in the family, left all my stuff with my roommate, and took off. And now . . ."

Oh, what was I to say? Just leaving like that. What could I offer him, to make up for what he was doing? "But that's your future."

"The future won't go away." He leaned over and kissed me. "I found you—that's the only thing that matters. Anyway, I'm starved." He still had hold of my hand and was urging me forward.

Near the entrance of the side street, we caught the smell of food, then saw a vendor's stand. "That's the second thing that matters, at least right now."

We wove our way through to the line of people waiting. After we'd bought tamales, cups of chili, and cups of lemonade, we headed towards the park. It was not so crowded as before, and we found a shady spot under an acacia tree with all its reddish tassels. I had worked up quite an appetite myself. We spread out our little feast. We dug in. The tamales were filled with chicken and green chili. I tried to eat slowly, they were so good.

"I still can't believe you've come here—for me. You must go back and . . ."

He shrugged. "First we have to see about you. The future can wait—it's always there. Your future too."

I wanted to believe him. To see something beyond all that had happened, all that had been torn apart. How do you stand up again when you've hit the dust in pieces? . . . That's what I wanted to know. You have to pull yourself up—nobody can do it for you, even with all your longing. Billy had taught me a few things about appearance and disappearance, even though he painted new dreams before my eyes. Only he wasn't in the world—I'd never see him again.

"It's true," Ben insisted, as he told me again how much he admired me—what I could do.

"The snakes? I just took advantage of what was offered. Jessie was a lucky chance. I had nothing else."

"That's just the thing," he said. "But she brought out your talent—something real you couldn't fake. And even more. You had to know what you were doing. You had to make something out of yourself, and it was beautiful to watch."

"Jessie can do it so much better. I didn't even come close."

"You know better than that," he said. "Come on now. Give yourself some credit. It took you above everything surrounding you." He reached for my hand again.

At least he didn't think it was just about me trying to be sexy—just having all the guys getting their jollies while the booze loosened up their wallets. "Anyway, I don't want to look at another snake," I said. "Not after what happened." I could feel the tears gathering.

"They're trying to convict the Reverend and some of his pals for arson," Ben said. "When I got there the town was up in arms."

"It won't bring Billy back."

"But it might save the town."

I hadn't thought of that, of the people I'd loved there and what they were trying to create. I wanted to be happy with Ben, not to let in all the grief to spoil things. "Do forgive me," I said. "You're here, and I can't tell you what that means."

"No need to try. Just being with you . . ." I leaned over and kissed him. We kissed again.

We gathered up our cups and papers, took them to the trash bin and strolled away from where the families camped to where I'd seen Priam in all his glory. Couples still sat on their blankets putting bites of food into each other's mouths, kissing, making toasts, and drinking their wine. Food and wine, joy and lovemaking under the trees. You wanted to lose yourself there forever.

Ben led me away from the path, to a sheltered spot. We lay back in the grass and he moved beside me, put his arms around me, and planted kisses as I tried to speak. His touch awakened all the sensations that had fed my longing when I first knew him and which sprang up whenever I thought of the Kitty Kat. How sweet it was to feel his kisses on my neck, my breasts, the touch of his tongue. And how could I resist lovemaking once again—just once more?

Afterwards, out of breath after a long kiss, we separated like two drunken bees.

He was eager to go on, but I had to stop him before I was swallowed up. "Wait, please wait. There's so much to settle."

"You must know what I feel about you."

I put my finger to his lips. "You hardly know me," I said. "You don't know where I've been, all that's happened to me. All that bites me in two. I don't know yet what to do with it all. We hardly know each other."

Maybe that was what Jessie meant. Maybe I still didn't know myself either. Was I just clinging to someone for rescue? If what I felt wasn't love, what was it? Just these two bodies . . . I couldn't believe that was all. Yet . . .

"But when you go back . . . Your future . . . And your father . . ." I said it as softly as I could.

He sat up. "Yes, my father . . . I love the guy, believe me. He's had to be father and mother to me all these years. I know what he wants for me—he wants the best. And my mother, too, if she were still alive. I don't know if she'd want the same. He's got it all worked out in his head. Study law. Get hold of power. Power is the thing with him. Make the world different. I don't knock it. But I want to go another way." His expression changed. "Anyway, I love you."

"But if you throw everything away . . ."

"You know I'm not going to do that."

And what would his father think of me? Something he'd picked up in the street. "And maybe if you knew all that's happened to me—how low I sank."

"I don't care—you're still the same, I'm sure of it. I've had the advantages. Maybe you think that's all there is to me. That I can't find my own way . . ."

Maybe I was afraid he'd throw me aside after the shine wore off. Seems like I knew the world better than he did. His father had his dreams, too. Not for his son to pick up some little slut. And from what Jessie told me he wasn't about to give way. There was Ben trying to magic the future while I struggled in spite of all I felt for him.

"I tell you what," I said, standing up. "This is the Carnival, the biggest fiesta I've ever seen, and we haven't even gotten into it yet. Let's do that and see what happens."

"Don't you love me?" he said, in his frog voice, with an exaggerated droop of his shoulders.

"Of course I love you, you idiot. Ever since we first got together."

"That says it. That's why I came—for love. Let's just go our way while the getting's good."

It was so tempting just to let him lead me away. And I admit I was putting things off. But some impulse was pushing up at me, and it wouldn't let me be in peace.

"Marry me."

"Oh, Ben, I can't just leap in right this minute. I'm all torn up inside. And you—what about you? What do you want to be?"

"Anything you like. I just want you."

"That's not what I mean. It's not what I like."

"Can't you trust me?"

I looked at him as if I hadn't seen him before. Trust him with my life when I could hardly trust myself?

In the distance I heard chimes—silvery, like water shining with late afternoon sun. They reminded me of laughter that comes in a moment of sudden joy, just bubbling up. They spoke of what I felt just having Ben there beside me. Like I'd once felt when I was dancing. It was fiesta time. Soon it would be twilight, the crowning of the King and Queen. There was something yet to do.

"There's someone I need to meet. Selena, she's called, the Mistress of Mysteries. She'll take us to get a costume."

"A costume?" he said. "You really want to get into that?"

"Please do it with me," I said. "Almost everybody gets into it. Maybe it matters."

171

He laughed a little sadly. "Okay by me—only I'm just afraid I'll lose you."

I tried to smile at him. It was hard to let him go. "Whatever happens, that won't ever happen."

"That's like some kind of riddle."

"It's one for me, too." I took his hand as we walked from the park towards the building where I was supposed to meet Selena.

"Where will we meet again?"

"You found me—I'll find you. Somehow we'll find each other." Then, *If we're supposed to*, I thought, and a chill went through me.

"You're sure of that?" He stepped in front of me so that I had to stop and look him in the eye.

"If there's anything I'm sure of, it's that."

He shook his head. "You're not saying no."

"Of course not. When it's time, it'll be yes."

"When it's time . . . Oh, Grace."

As we moved towards the building with all its brilliant tiles, I saw that various scenes were painted on them, some bright with sunlight, others in darker colors with shadowy images. And they kept changing. Just before we got there, a tall man dressed as a courtier, wig and all, approached Ben and invited him to follow him towards one of the costume rooms.

Ben stood for a moment as though he hadn't quite made up his mind.

"It's part of the magic," the courtier said. "You wouldn't want to miss the chance. We encourage everybody, but of course it's up to you."

Ben looked at me, laughed and said, "Okay, I'm game."

I blew Ben a kiss as I saw Selena approach. I didn't feel exactly lighthearted. She smiled brightly as I turned to follow her.

XIV.

First the music caught me up—I melted into it. The flute rose up like a bird, calling you towards something that spirals up to a place you don't even know. It doesn't belong to you—it goes so far beyond you, you have no notion of where it disappears. Seizes you more than hunger or thirst. It keeps sending you upward till it feels like your skin doesn't fit—you just want to let go, even of your name and all you've ever been.

Then came the drums thrumming in, catching up the blood with a Come, Come, Come. Promising. Just telling you there's more, but down deep—there in the earth, more than you ever dreamed of. And you have to have them both. Clarinets and saxophones, waterfalls pouring over rocks. Then the solitary flute reminding you that you've got it all to do alone. The sounds carried me until I couldn't separate myself from them, outside and inside at once, music beating in my blood, taking me to a farther edge.

Selena took my hand—I had to watch where I was going. Stones and roots to stumble over. I saw people coming towards us dressed in costumes.

What costume would actually fit me? How could they manage the right one in the right size for everybody? They'd have to have a world full of them. I thought of all the others who'd been thronging the streets and the park, some dressed as lions or turtles, others dressed as crows or dogs, butterflies or hummingbirds; all sorts of other creatures, including those that crept and crawled. Then all the notes of the human scale: athletes and gypsies, drunks and warriors, clowns, kings and queens, holy men and women; old and young; others with childish faces; men dressed as women, and women as men. There were still all those waiting to get into their costumes for the great event of the evening, the crowning of the King of the Sun and the Queen of the Moon.

Selena must have sensed the questions brewing in my mind.

173

"You're wondering, aren't you, why we go to such trouble to see that everyone is in costume?" she said. "The festival is such a special time—people coming from all over the territory, rejoicing in the chance to leave the daily grind. For you know, they get sick of it—stale as moldy cheese. Deep down, they're itching for something to happen—an adventure to talk about the rest of the year. And maybe to come back and do things differently. Get out of the old patterns, old nightmares, old ruts, open their eyes to something new. You know how we get buried in our hurts and disappointments, how they become our obsessions so we can't see beyond them . . . Can't move. We can't . . ." She put her hand up to her face. "Things have changed for me," she said in a low voice. "You can't imagine, nor could I. Oh, the darkness you get chained in—the blindness! But here . . ."

Hard for me to imagine—that putting on another kind of outfit would make all that much difference. Wear red and you'll hit the sky. Blue—take yourself down a notch.

"Would it matter if I dressed up to look like Princess Grace or the Queen of Sheba? Make me feel I was the Royal Wonder? Or Little Orphan Annie? Maybe that would fit better."

"You'll see. The costumes make something happen," she said. Then she corrected herself. "No . . . It's being here in a certain costume that makes things happen, draws certain elements up into light and air."

She intrigued me, made the old curiosity rise up. And the closer we got to the building, the more I could see the scenes in the tiles: men and women working, building houses, cleaning, sewing, cooking; women nursing their babies; families sitting around the dinner table; birds across the sky—celebrations and games, dances and races. Then the scene would brighten or darken, and there were couples walking in the moonlight; children playing games, sitting around a fire . . . So they played, light and dark, some things fearful and full of anger and violence. I could almost hear shouts and cries.

I was being jostled by a wind that had come up, blowing around us, making its own kind of music and noise, sometimes moaning, sometimes soft, promising and wooing me. I was giddy with it all. It carried a voice that whispered in my ear. *Enter the doorway and you'll never be the same. Everything is possible.* It scared me and elated me. Selena smiled as I stood speechless.

I had no idea whether a voice actually spoke—or if I'd imagined it. What it said sounded real enough, but how could I be different? Another voice, deep in me, whispered, *What has happened can't be undone or changed. And that is what you are—under a curse.*

Something in me wanted to scoff at everything and kick and yell out that all of it was just a bad joke. My whole life even. A trick of appearances. I wanted to turn and run, but the hand that held mine was firm, encouraging, and it wasn't going to let go. I saw that Selena had yellow eyes edged with green, and her smile assured me. As I continued, the wind grew softer and gradually fell away.

In front of us was a large doorway where panels of light ran in streams, joining and separating, swirling and changing colors. A circle of light played around everyone as well, shifting colors, bright and dull.

People wandered in, chatting, then paused to marvel at this year's display.

"Too bad they take it all down," a stocky, bearded man said to his companion. "And it's never the same two years in a row."

"Well, I've had nearly the same costume for three years in a row," said a woman, maybe in her forties, who looked like she had just stepped out of a fashion magazine. "I'm getting tired of it. I wonder why they don't give me a new one."

"Because you're the same little minx you've always been, dressing up your dolls and pouting when you don't get your way."

"You prick!"

Her companion paused to laugh at her, "You'll never change, darling," he pronounced in his deep voice. "Maybe that's what I love about you."

"Get out of my sight before I slap you."

"I was merely telling you the truth, my pigeon."

"I'll truth you." She raised her arm as though for a strike. "I can tell you a few things too."

I began to think the whole costume business was more complicated than I imagined. But then, with all those people . . . It occurred to me that the couple about to kill each other might be enjoying themselves.

"Wait a moment," Selena said, as I started to follow them. "That's one way many people choose. There are a lot of advantages," she said, "but there's another. You can decide for yourself."

There was music playing, different from what I'd been hearing. "Listen a bit." It was jaunty. Guitars, the percussion and brass were boisterous and full of sound. The music kept building till sound and rhythm took over, kept repeating and growing louder, more confused, till I thought my eardrums would split. I put my hands to my ears. But then it fell away and the music became calm, placid, the same tune repeated over and over.

"The other way isn't easier. Maybe even more difficult. I can't really say how it will be for you. Or anything about it really. Some find it very hard, and they have to turn around—maybe wait and come back another year. Or not. And some, I for one, found great rewards."

I was thinking of Ben, wondering what he would choose. Somehow I was sure he wouldn't settle for something easy. I could see he'd had loss and struggle.

Selena was pointed in another direction. "The other doorway is over there."

I couldn't make it out from among the trees. My head was a confused jumble. Why did everything have to be so complicated? What if I'd done it all wrong, the way I'd let him go? I tried not to think so. And I couldn't do less than I'd asked him to do.

I turned in the direction she'd pointed towards. When she saw I was willing, she turned us into a path that continued on into the trees. I saw that some part of the building had been set into the rocks on the side of a hill, and she showed me where to look for the entrance. Finally, I saw it—you had to know what you were looking for. A glow from the rocks with their moss gave its own kind of light.

"We'll go in here." I didn't see her signal or press a button. But a stronger light came up, the colors brightening as the doorway opened and then closed behind us. It was like standing in a theater after the movie is over, the crowd gone, and you're there alone. Only the show wasn't over.

The space was filled with stars like it held a piece of the night sky. Various spaces opened out, some with trees and flowering shrubs. As we walked, we were in the middle of a summer evening with blinking stars and fireflies.

I tried to ask questions, but Selena interrupted.

"Let me show you." She led me sometimes by the elbow, sometimes by the hand, pointing out a few of those who were coming, newly dressed in their costumes.

"Do you choose your costume?"

"Oh, yes," she said, "only you might not know for a while how it came to be yours."

What sort of riddle was this? Had I ever really known what I was choosing, or did things just happen to me? Was all this real? How could it be? If I couldn't still feel my hand in Selena's, I would have said I'd dreamed it up. I was hardly real to myself. I was here in the moment, but where had I come from? Where had I begun? I didn't even know who my mother and father were. Did it matter? Would I be anything different if I knew?

We were in a brightly lit passage we'd entered through the trees. The walls were decorated with photos and paintings of men, women, and children in various poses and costumes, and fans, hats, masks, and shoes from past fiestas were hanging alongside them. A large doorway opened to a great room with several long heavy wooden tables, piled high with masks, hats, parts of costumes, and bolts of cloth. Around them groups of men and woman sat or stood, commenting, sometimes laughing or exclaiming, as they sorted the items, held them up, examined them. One of the women smiled at me when she saw Selena and said, "Selena hoped you'd be coming," then handed me what looked like the mask of a child, then another, a third—four in all.

"These are for you."

"Come," Selena said, leading me down the passage into a smaller room. "You can try them out, see what happens. I'll be back soon."

The room was dimly lit from above with small circles of light.

When I put on the kid mask, I was in a meadow, where a little girl was picking flowers. Seemed like I knew her; yet she was a stranger, too. There were flowers all around, morning glories and dessert poppies, paintbrush, and chamissa. And tall grasses. I wanted to gather a bouquet. I could hear a song—someone was singing it to me: *Baa, baa, black sheep—have you any wool?* Felt like somebody was poking me in the chest at the same time. *Little black sheep is you. Little black sheep.* Someone laughed, and I giggled. But the light disappeared suddenly and I heard a sound like thunder. The meadow became a sea of shadow. A shock went through the ground, and the air tasted bitter. I wailed and started to run as rain came pelting down. Something was chasing me, big like a bull or an ogre, with a dark human face. *Selena, come help me.* It was a struggle to get through the grasses and roots. They snatched at me as I ran and stumbled.

The breath was out of me, a stitch in my side. Trembling, just trembling, I stooped down under a bush and cowered as a heavy drumming rushed past. I was still there, still alive . . . The aliveness grew inside me . . . holding onto me. For a moment I thought I saw Antoinette, running up ahead, and I took off after her. Ralph's face flickered past me. Then the Kid and I were sitting there on the rocks in the arroyo telling our stories.

It was quiet now, at the edge of the meadow. When I took off the mask, I was back in the room where I started. I stared down at the second mask lying on the table.

Hesitantly, I took it up, examined it. It was a mask that made me think of a boy not quite grown. And that's what I felt like when I put it on. Me riding my bicycle into town and wangling a way to get to the circus. Getting past Priam to where I wanted to be. Spending the money in my pocket. And here came Jessie with her snakes. I was still a boy-person, still roaming. I felt the freedom of it. It was a hidden thing. But I'd had a dose of it, even though a dark shadow threatened at the edge of it. Sometimes I could push it away, but deep down I was afraid.

A woman stared at me from the third mask, and there was something in her face that made me afraid. She wanted to lure me into an unknown space that she knew all about. I found myself in a room where people were playing a game of masks, changing from one face into another. A crowd of players were gathered at tables, playing cards and throwing dice. Other people stood at an auction block bidding on various creatures, strange ones with human faces but with bodies of birds or animals. A woman was holding a monkey close to her breast. I wanted to turn away and yet they were fascinating too.

Mirrors lined the walls on all sides, taking your face and making it long or squinching it up. Funny, but ugly too. All the faces there kept melting from one into another, so that you couldn't tell if any of them belonged to the person wearing them. A lot of laughter. Hoots of surprise. I saw myself in all the different faces like I could be any of them.

From their midst, a fortune-teller handed me a card with a man's face on the front. "Wanted," it said underneath. And as I looked at the card, the man winked.

"Am I sexy enough for you?" he drawled. Maybe I'd seen someone like him at the Kitty Kat or The Olde Black Magic, but I didn't recognize him. Something pulled me towards him but at the same time repelled me. I had to back away right quick.

"You think you're too good for me? I'll be right there to catch you when I can," and he disappeared from the card before I could say, "You've got it all wrong."

"Lots of good fish in the sea," the fortune-teller said, laughing. "Catch the one you want—don't let him get away. Maybe you'll want them all."

I looked around for Selena, but I couldn't see her.

Who do you think you are? A clown was dancing in front of me, or so it looked. Dancing naked, stripes, red and black and white all over his body, with a tail decorated with black and white rings. A costume he could have been born with. Had he been in the parade? He wore a white mask. He danced and smirked, making vulgar gestures, teasing me. With a shit-eating grin, he swiped the rings off his tail and threw them on the ground. *How's that for style?*

You think you can get out of this? How come you're here anyway?

179

You're getting out of hand. Breaking the rules. You'll be fined.

"I'm sorry," I said, though I had nothing to apologize for. "I was led here."

No apologies, the clown yelled. *No excuses. I don't accept them.*

I got angry then. "I have just as much right to be here as you do. Go stand on your head," I yelled. "Go bite your tail. Do your tricks and get lost."

Atta girl. He was laughing like he couldn't stop. Tickled. *Knew I could get a rise out of you.* He turned and waggled his behind, whipped his tail around and ran off, roaring with laughter. *Hey, I'll bet she'd slap me. Hey, she's a fiery one. Hot stuff.*

Then I was laughing, too.

I thought I'd passed some kind of test, but suddenly a crowd pushed in, bodies and faces pressing around me. I could smell their sweat and body odors. A sea of flesh. Pushing and shoving, heavy, shadowy, dark. I couldn't move. Pressing, squeezing me. Until I was shoved into a pit, going deeper. Screaming in the dark—a shower of stones fell. It seemed the end of me. I closed my eyes and tried to find some little spark. I prayed for it. I put everything I had into holding onto whatever small thing lived—it was so precious. I took a breath, then another.

This time unseen hands removed the mask, and I felt the bright little chip glowing inside. A diamond. A diamond blazing. I'd found my way to it again. This time I could really hear Billy's voice as though it had finally reached inside me.

I stood with a blindfold over my eyes, a glass in my hand.

"Drink some of this—it will help you forward," a voice told me. Someone taking me by the hand and leading me on unsteady feet. Then I stood blinking in a dim light and was given another mask to put on, sometimes more like a woman, sometimes more of an animal. It looked very strange to me.

I was standing on a balcony, looking out over a garden full of flowers with the fresh scents of carnations and daisies, roses and lilies, yellow, red, pink, and white. I wanted desperately to be down with them, the space appeared so inviting. I looked around me for a way to go down. But when I looked back, things had become cloudy. The air was full of smoke, like cigarette smoke. The air began to reek with the odor Priam gave off—from booze and tobacco and unwashed flesh. The stink of his whole existence. The boozy air filled with cigarette smoke. Like the air surrounding those people I danced for. Valdemar's gold tooth gleaming in his grin.

When I looked down into the garden, a black dog was digging up the lilies. "Go! Get out!" I rushed from the balcony and found the steps down into the garden, grabbed a stick I saw on the ground, and started beating the creature. I kept beating and beating it until it escaped and ran off yelping. I stood trembling at what I'd done. How could I? I couldn't believe it was me. Who had done it—how could it be me? A terrible moment. I started sobbing. I wept for a long time, knowing the terrible rage that had exploded inside me and what I'd done to that dog. Then I wept for all that had happened to me and those around me. Not just Billy—but Alta and the Kid, and Dusty. Maybe even Donovan and Curran had suffered just from being who they were. Others came to mind—Nellie and Louise and Bama, the cook, the other girls at the Kitty Kat and the life they led. It seemed like I was weeping for all those I didn't know and would never meet, but who were suffering and sick and lonely and down on their luck.

I was alone but I became aware of voices murmuring around me.

From below, a melody was taking shape out of a storm of sound, and a little way off a figure stood playing a blue guitar. She, too, was all in blue and the guitar was covered all in different mosaics of blue, shifting from one to another—now a fiery blue that gave a strange and wonderful light to the trees. Playing a tune I knew, that teased me—where had it come from? Haunting me, but refusing to give its name. I thought of Ben, of making love—of loving,

Words formed in my mind, a song someone might have been singing—just briefly, then it was gone. I kept listening for the singing. I had to listen for it, for those faint words that just barely touched my ear. How could I live without them?

I pulled off the mask and was back again in the room. Selena came this time with several women, and they took me to a bathing pool and let me relax in water like silk with flower petals floating on the surface. They handed me a cup of cider and left me to loll and drink the warm liquid. Then the women helped me to dry off and dress.

"Come," Selena said, "It's time to get your costume. We'll go to the fitting room, You can see how these costumes come together. I've always found it an exciting place."

She opened a door to a huge room, all lit up, full of busy people. We were in the midst of talk and laughter, the whir of sewing machines. There were fewer people working here, but still there were a number of men and women, busy cutting, sewing, and holding up costumes and masks and trying them on those who stood on various platforms scattered about. Many of these had been chosen from racks of finished costumes that lined the room. Others were being fashioned for those who wanted new ones.

"Some of these people have been doing this for many years," Selena said. 'They're true artists—you can't imagine how much they know by now."

She took me to one of the platforms and pulled a curtain around me so that I stood inside an oddly shaped area where three women were ready to measure and cut and sew. They took off my clothes to compare with some of the outfits on the racks and then started fitting me with my costume. The bra of silver and red glittered with little flecks of gold woven in, and the trousers were a figured gold cloth with a short filmy skirt on top that hugged the hips. They uncovered a basket beside their worktable and with awe and nervous laughter held up two albino pythons. And how was it they were there, these snakes?

"We've never had to do this before," one of them said. "Horses yes; dogs and cats, and even a lion cub once. But what are we doing with snakes?"

Two young albino pythons, silvery streaks themselves, beauties both of them. I held one in each hand, then let them settle on my shoulders. I began to feel that special bond I'd known before, something that lived in my blood and brought us together. *The snakes know the way*, a voice reminded me. Selena led me to a pavilion where a crowd of people were waiting for the spectacle to unfold.

A little distance from me, closer to the river, was another dais Selena pointed to. There stood two crowned figures in splendid costumes—the King of the Sun and Queen of the Moon, the king in red, the queen in white, covered with suns and moons of the opposite colors. Alta and Dusty. I recognized them immediately. Royalty! My heart leapt—how about that? King and Queen of the fiesta standing there, with their golden scepters, ready to start the show.

A slow undulating music began—the spotlight was on me, and the snakes started to tell me how to move and how we were to create the dance together. A surge of energy and joy ran through me. What was alive in me had taken shape with them. And I was back in the roadside zoo with Antoinette and Caruso. I was dancing them, dancing the other animals as well, dancing what I felt in them and meeting myself in them. They came alive again in all their wildness and I knew the wild part of myself. All part of the dance. And Ralph, too. And then the Kid and his Mama, and even Priam, because they'd been part of my life. And Jessie, who had loved and fostered me, and the girls. And Ben, who'd given me a taste of a different kind of love. And all of the Carnival. I couldn't even leave out those who had harmed me—they were part of my life—and I had to dance them away before I could hold myself steady and take a new shape. All the while we kept moving, the snakes and I, as they brought me to something deeper than what I'd lived and known, past days and weeks, past all time, to a deeper place inside. I was losing myself in it, just letting the dance take me where it was going when a voice yelled out, "Grace!" like an arrow aimed for a target.

The old bugger had found his way here. But I didn't miss a beat—there was a power in me now to push him away. Suddenly I saw him drop to his knees staring wildly as though he'd seen a ghost. *Billy, is that you?* He lifted up his hands as though in prayer, as though he was praying for his life. *Well,* I thought, *now you know what it's like . . .* Dear life—all the threat had leaked out of him, and I was free to continue the dance.

Gladys Swan has published five novels, *Carnival for the Gods*, (Vintage Contemporaries Series), *Ghost Dance: A Play of Voices*, (LSU Press, nominated for the PEN/Faulkner Award), *A Dark Gamble*, *Ancestors*, and *Small Wonder*, as well as seven collections of short fiction. Her poetry and essays, and short stories have appeared in many literary magazines and anthologies. Much of her work is set in New Mexico, where she grew up. Though she has spent most of her career as a writer, she has devoted much of her time during the last two decades to painting and exploring the creative process. She was the first writer since the inception of the Vermont Studio Center to receive a fellowship for a residency in painting. She also received a fellowship from the Lilly Endowment for a year's study of Inuit art and mythology and a Fulbright Award as a writer-in-residence in Yugoslavia. Her paintings have appeared as the cover art for various literary magazines and books, including the most recently published, *The Tiger's Eye: New & Selected Stories*. She has twice been a Guest Writer at the Vermont Studio Center and has held residencies at Yaddo, the Chateau de Lavigny in Switzerland. the Fimdacion Valparaiso in Spain and others. She has taught literature and creative writing at various colleges and universities, notably, in the MFA Program at the Vermont College of the Arts and at the University of Missouri-Columbia. She received an Honorary Doctorate of Humane Letters from Western New Mexico University and gave the commencement address. *The Carnival Quintet*, an outgrowth of her first novel, is being published by Serving House Books. The first volume, *Carnival for the Gods*, appeared in September, 2014. She has done the cover paintings for the series.